THE CHAMPAK STORY BOX

RUPA

Published by
Rupa Publications India Pvt. Ltd 2021
7/16, Ansari Road, Daryaganj
New Delhi 110002

Sales Centres:
Allahabad Bengaluru Chennai
Hyderabad Jaipur Kathmandu
Kolkata Mumbai

ISBN: 978-93-91256-29-6

Fourth impression 2022

10 9 8 7 6 5 4

Printed in India

TABLE OF CONTENTS

TABLE of CONTENTS

 FUN   DISCOVERY   FITTING IN

DETERMINATION   RATIONALITY

THE TREE OF JALEBIS

By Harendra Chakravorty

Blacky the Bear had just spent two hours breaking down a honeycomb from the **highest** branches of a tree. He had worked hard for the **HONEY** he was taking home. On his way home, he passed Vicky the Vixen's house. He knew how much Vicky loved honey, and decided he would share some with her.

"Vicky, see what I've got for you," shouted Blacky, banging on Vicky's door.

"Who is this **BANGING** on my door?" shouted Vicky from inside. "That's a sandalwood door made to order and it cost me hundreds of dollars!" Saying that, she came to the door. "Oh Blacky! Welcome, welcome," she exclaimed.

BLACKY SHARES WITH CARE

"Whenever Blacky comes, he brings something good to eat. I wonder what he's got today!" she thought to herself, ushering Blacky into the dining room and taking out two bowls.

Blacky laughed. "How did you know I had brought you honey?" he asked. "You brought out the bowls even before

I could **open** my bag!"

Vicky **LAUGHED** too. "Oh Blacky, don't tease me. I can smell honey from 100 kilometres away!"

Blacky took out the honey, and put it into one of the bowls. The other bowl was covered. Vicky picked that bowl up, opened it, and offered Blacky something he had never seen before. "Vicky always gets interesting things from the city," thought Blacky to himself.

"What are these strange orange things?" asked Blacky curiously.

"I have never seen such tangled round things!"

"Take one and eat," encouraged Vicky.

"Why, there's honey oozing from it!" exclaimed Blacky, picking one up.

"These SWEETS© are called jalebis, and that's sugar syrup oozing from it. I'm sure you'd never have eaten something so delicious!" said Vicky.

Blacky ate a jalebi and **agreed** it was the most delicious thing he had eaten. "I can give you ten of these," said Vicky. "But in return, I want all your honey!" Blacky readily agreed, and ran home with his jalebis.

Blacky enjoyed the jalebis so much, he decided to make a deal with Vicky. He would give her honey regularly in exchange for jalebis. Vicky readily agreed, and Blacky worked extra hard to collect honey from the **TALLEST** trees, just so he could have a regular supply of jalebis.

After a week or so, Blacky thought he would ask Vicky more about where these delicious jalebis came from. He walked down to Vicky's house and realised she was setting off on a journey. There was a **large** drum placed outside her house, and she was bringing her car close to it. "Vicky, where are you off to? And what's in this drum?" asked Blacky curiously.

"Oh, it's some stuff I'm taking for my sister who lives in the Amazon jungle," said Vicky. "She is not well, so I thought I would go visit her." Saying that, Vicky loaded the drum into the car. "But tell me, Blacky, what brings you here? Have you **BrOUGHt** me more honey?

"Oh no. I couldn't get much honey today. I just came to ask you where you get those delicious jalebis from," said Blacky.

Vicky wasn't expecting this question. She thought for a while and then said: "Oh, Blacky, these jalebis **grow** on trees that are found in the Amazon jungle!"

SECRET JUNGLE OF JALEBIS

Blacky nodded, and watched Vicky **DRIVE** away. He then walked home thoughtfully.

As he reached his house, he saw Cheeku the Rabbit walking by, **MUNCHING** on a carrot. Cheeku was the most intelligent animal in Champakvan, and was always studying.

"Hello, Cheeku! I haven't seen you for a while," said Blacky.

"Yes, Blacky, I have been to the Amazon jungle to do some **research.** on some rare plants that are found only there," explained Cheeku.

Blacky's face lit up. "Did you eat a lot of jalebis there?" he asked **EAGERLY**. "There must be thousands of jalebi trees in the Amazon jungle!"

Cheeku laughed when he heard this, thinking Blacky was **joking**. "What do you mean by jalebi trees? Anyone can make jalebis and they are available at almost every restaurant, though I have not seen any near Champakvan."

Blacky was stunned. He told Cheeku what Vicky had claimed. Neither of them could understand why Vicky had told Blacky such a story. Cheeku decided to get Vicky to tell the **truth.** He told Blacky his plan and the two went home.

A few days later, Cheeku and Blacky walked towards Vicky's house and saw Vicky driving up. She **stopped** the car and leaned out. "Blacky! I did not expect to see you today. Did you bring honey? I'm afraid I have no jalebis for you right now!"

Blacky shook his head. "I don't need jalebis from you anymore, Vicky. I have the seeds of a jalebi tree. Now I will have a jalebi tree in my garden!" Saying that, he showed Vicky a handful of orange **candies**.

"Don't be silly! There's no such thing as jalebi seeds," scoffed Vicky.

"Why not?" asked Cheeku. "If there are jalebi trees, there must be jalebi **SEEDS!** How else will the trees grow?"

Vicky looked ashamed. She admitted that she had been selling the honey Blacky had collected and had bought him jalebis from the city in **EXCHANGE**. The honey was in great demand in other forests because Blacky collected only the best. "I'm sorry, Blacky. I lied to you about the jalebis, because I knew if you started buying them from the city, I would not get any more honey to sell. Please **FORGIVE** me," said Vicky. She offered Blacky the money she had got for the honey, and quickly drove away.

Blacky looked sad, realising that he should not blindly trust anyone. "Come on, Blacky," said Cheeku, trying to **CHEER** him up. "Let's go home. I'll teach you how to make jalebis!" Blacky laughed and followed his friend home, ready to learn something new.

DOCTOR WATCH

By Kumud Kumar

Buzo the Monkey was *fond* of buying the latest watches. One morning when he was reading the newspaper, he saw an advertisement about the launch of a new smartwatch that could check the **Heart** rate when worn.

He was fascinated and immediately left his house to go buy the watch.

On his way, he met Meenu the Goat. "Buzo, where are you going so early in the morning?" she asked.

"Meenu, a new doctor watch has been launched. I am going to the shop to buy it," replied Buzo excitedly.

"Doctor watch?" asked Meenu, **curiously.**

"Yes, a doctor watch! I can't explain just now. I've got to reach the shop first," said Buzo hurrying away, leaving Meenu's question unanswered.

Meenu too walked away wondering what Buzo had been talking about.

Buzo reached the shop and asked for the watch. The shopkeeper explained the features and functioning of the ⌚ **WATCH** to Buzo. "Not only does the watch show time, date and temperature, it also checks the blood sugar, blood pressure and heart rate of the person wearing it," he boasted. Buzo immediately bought the watch for ₹700.

He wore the watch and left the shop. He couldn't wait to show it off to his friends. On his way home, he saw them *playing* in the park. Instead of running to meet them, he strolled in the park and repeatedly checked the time on his watch.

SHOW OFF BUZO!

Tintin the Squirrel saw him wearing the **BRIGHT** and shiny watch and asked, "Buzo, have you just bought a new watch? Is that why you are checking the time on it repeatedly?"

Embarrassed, Buzo replied, "Yes, Tintin, I bought this watch just now. It is a doctor watch and is different from all the other watches I own."

"It looks great. Can I see?" asked Tintin as she took a closer *look.*

Soon, Buzo was surrounded by his friends as they all wanted to see his doctor watch. Buzo boasted about the functions of the watch. He pressed the **BUTT⦿NS** and the colourful display impressed them.

"Buzo, your watch looks amazing. Since it has such great

features, why don't you show us what it says about your health?" asked Kannu the Elephant.

"Sure. I'll measure my blood sugar right away," said Buzo.

"How does it do that?" Kannu asked.

"If I press this button, it tells me my blood sugar," said Buzo and pressed it.

"Wow!" the animals **EXCLAIMED** as they saw numbers changing on the watch.

The watch buzzed when it was done calculating. "Right now, my sugar is at 360," said Buzo with pride.

"360! That is way too high. Even my grandfather, who has diabetes, does not have such **HIGH** blood sugar. We have to admit you to a hospital right away," exclaimed Kannu.

Buzo was not familiar with blood sugar levels and was taken aback when he realised his sugar was not at a normal level.

Tintin then said, "Buzo, I think you should check your blood **PRESSURE** too."

Buzo wasted no time and pressed the button to check his blood pressure. Everyone looked at his watch, which showed 180-110. Tintin's grandmother suffered from high blood pressure, so she knew what those levels meant.

ICU

PEAKiNG STRESS LEVELS

"Buzo, I think you should visit a doctor immediately. This is a warning sign, you better hurry," she said.

Now, Buzo was scared.

"If this is the case, check your heart rate too," suggested Larry the Giraffe.

Buzo's watch displayed a heart rate of 140 per minute.

Larry was **SHOCKED**. "This is higher than normal, let's go to the doctor," he said.

Buzo lost all hope and felt **DIZZY**. Before he could make it to the doctor's clinic, he fainted.

The animals picked him up and **RAN** to Dr Dobby's clinic.

The doctor became worried seeing so many animals coming towards his clinic. He saw Buzo was unconscious and immediately called for a stretcher and carried him inside.

"Please save me, doctor," Buzo muttered, opening his eyes.

"Children, please do not **WORRY**. Tell me what happened? Did Buzo have an injury?" the doctor asked.

"No, doctor. But his blood sugar is at 360, his blood pressure 180-110 and his heart rate is at 140 per minute," Kannu told him.

"Oh, that is serious! I'll take him to the emergency room," said Dr Dobby and rushed Buzo in.

The other animals waited outside the door.

Dr Dobby checked Buzo's pulse and found it to be normal.

Then, he checked his blood pressure, which again was normal at 120-80. The blood sugar figures also came out to be NORMAL at 110. "Buzo, you're fine," said Dr Dobby and informed the other animals too.

Buzo jumped up when he heard this. "Am I really FINE, Doctor?"

"Yes, I examined your health and you are fine. But, tell me, who examined you before?" asked Dr Dobby.

"Doctor, Buzo was examined by doctor watch on his wrist," said Kannu, softly.

Now, Dr Dobby understood the situation and smiled. "You should not believe everything you see or hear until it is thoroughly DIAGNOSED by a doctor. The watch is just an electronic instrument, not a doctor. The numbers may not be accurate because Buzo doesn't know how to examine himself. For example, did he sit upright or sleep when checking his blood pressure and other readings?" asked the doctor.

Everyone nodded, including Buzo. They understood Dr Dobby's advice. Ever since, Buzo read the instructions carefully whenever he used something new!

PUZZLE TIME

⏱ WATCH CLOSELY

Buzo's watch is damaged. Look at his watch below and spot what is wrong with it.

Answer on the last page

THE VEHICLES OF GOD

By Anupam Pardeshi

The spread of literacy in Vijayvan had not been *GOOD* for Pandit Bholaram the Monkey's business. He was no longer asked to read palms to predict the **FUTURE**, or to perform rituals for good health, success in studies or for entering a new home. The animals of Vijayvan knew these practices did not guarantee anything, and only helped Bholaram make money.

"Business has been dull, my friend," he told Bunty the Monkey, who had come to visit.

"A week has passed since I have had any customers, said Bholaram."

"Yes. Everyone has become wiser since the opening of the new **LIBRARY**," agreed Bunty.

"Please sit, Bunty. Let me get some tea for you," said Bholaram.

Bunty sat, looked around, and saw a book near him. The book was called 'Gods and Their Favourite Rides', and was all about the favourite vehicles of gods with **COLOURFUL** images. Bunty flipped through the book by the time Bholaram came back with the tea.

"Bholaram, I may have an 💡 **iDEA** that will help your business," he said. "There is another forest, somewhat far from here, called Devvan. The people there are uneducated and very superstitious. I think your business will do well there!"

Bholaram looked questioningly at Bunty. "I got an idea after going through this book," explained Bunty, and told Bholaram his idea. Hearing it, Bholaram became **EXCiTED.**

"Since I came up with this idea, I should be an equal partner. Give me half of what you earn," said Bunty. Bholaram agreed and both left for Devvan.

WHAT AN iDEA!

When they reached Devvan, they took a house on rent and hung a board outside. The board read 'Pandit Bholaram's Obstacle Removal Centre'. Word **spread** that a renowned pandit had come to Devvan, and the animals began gathering at the centre. Very soon, there was a crowd outside.

Motu the Owl was the first to go in. Touching Bholaram's feet, Motu said, "These days my earnings are not sufficient. Please suggest a way to increase them."

"What are you saying, Motu? Such a thing is not **POSSIBLE!** You are the carrier of Goddess Lakshmi herself! How can you suffer? This cannot happen to you!" Bholaram exclaimed.

"Who is Goddess Lakshmi?" asked Motu.

"You don't know about Goddess Lakshmi? She is the goddess of wealth who grants money to all. She rides on your back whenever she has to go somewhere," explained Bholaram.

This was all very **confusing** for Motu. Bholaram then

looked at his partner Bunty for support. Bunty took out the 📖**BOOK** and turned some pages. He showed an image to Motu and said, "Look, this is you and this is Goddess Lakshmi riding on you as she goes to visit a poor man to shower her blessings."

"Oh yes! That is me for sure! I never knew this," said Motu surprised.

"Worship Goddess Lakshmi and you will have so much money, you will never have to worry again," said Bunty.

This made Motu extremely **HAPPY**. He gave Pandit Bholaram some money for this knowledge and left.

Chuchu the Mouse came next. On seeing him, Bholaram said, "Why has Lord Ganesha's vehicle taken the pain of coming here? I would have visited your house if only you had asked me."

Bholaram's words did not mean anything to Chuchu. "I am having a *difficult* time these days. My wife and kids do not listen to me," he said.

"This is definitely the dark ages. Lord Ganesha's **RIDE** is having a difficult time! It is definitely not a good time," said Bholaram dramatically.

"I do not understand what you are saying about Lord Ganesha and me being his ride. Please tell me when my luck will change," said Chuchu impatiently.

Bunty showed Chuchu a picture from his book and explained. "Look, Lord Ganesha is riding on your back, on his task to remove problems for those who worship him."

Chuchu was **SURPRISED** to see that he was carrying Lord Ganesha on his back. This made him realise how great he was!

"Keep Lord Ganesha happy by worshipping him and soon everything will be back to normal," said Bunty.

Chuchu gave some **money** to Pandit Bholaram and left.

"Namaste, Pandit ji!" greeted Kalu the Crow, the next visitor. "I am never successful in any work I do. It seems as if there is an adverse influence of Lord Saturn on me."

"Lord Saturn can never affect you *adversely!* You are his ride. He can never let this happen to you!" Bholaram acted surprised.

Like always, Bunty took out his book and showed Kalu an image of a crow carrying Lord Saturn.

"Look, it is you who is carrying Lord Saturn! The Lord does not have wings to fly and he would be helpless without you. You should go and pray to him and you will be taken *CARE* of," said Bunty.

The list of animals visiting Bholaram was long. Bunty and Bholaram suggested that Ballu the Ox prayed to Lord Shiva;

Meenu the Peacock to Lord Kartikeya; Hansraj the Swan to Goddess Saraswati; and Golu the Eagle to Lord Vishnu. "These gods have to help their vehicles," they said. "**pray** 🙏 to them and your luck will turn."

Chuchu, Motu, Kalu, Ballu, Golu, Meenu, and all the others began worshipping their gods, and believed they would become wealthy and successful because of this.

After several days of praying when none of them got the desired results, they went back to Bholaram and complained, "Pandit ji, we have been worshipping our gods day and night but we have not been rewarded."

The huge crowd made Bholaram nervous. But the clever Bunty QUICKLY came up with an idea and said, "Don't worry, my friends! If you haven't succeeded in the simple method of prayer, then we will switch to a different and more complicated method. About five kilometres from here, there is a river. On its bank is a banyan tree. You should go there and start a hunger strike. Your strike will make the gods helpless and their work will come to a standstill. They will not be able to travel from one place to another," claimed Bunty.

The animals followed Bunty's advice and went to the river bank and sat under the **huge** banyan tree on a hunger strike. Two days passed but no god or goddess came to their rescue.

Rocky the Rabbit and Grandpa Elephant of Vijayvan were visiting Devvan. Grandpa had been carrying Rocky on his back, and was feeling tired. The two decided to rest beneath the banyan **TREE**.

"Rocky, let's rest here and have some food," said Grandpa. Rocky climbed down. The two looked at the large crowd gathered there. "What is this? It looks like all of Devvan is meeting here!" said Grandpa.

"Can't you see we are on a hunger strike? We will not eat or drink anything until God appears to help us," Kalu replied.

ONE FAILS, ANOTHER WINS

"I am Lord Ganesha's vehicle. Let me see how Lord Ganesha **MOVES** out of his house without me," Chuchu said proudly.

"I carry Goddess Lakshmi around. The Goddess sits proudly on me. Let me see how she manages without me," Motu added.

Grandpa and Rocky understood that animals had been fooled. They also noticed that the animals had become very **weak** from hunger. They were not even able to speak properly. Grandpa used his trunk to bring down the food hamper he was carrying on his back. The sweets and fruits in the hamper made the Devvan animals even more **HUNGRY**. Grandpa invited them to eat.

"No! We are on a hunger strike," they said together.

"But you all are the vehicles of the gods! How will they come to you if they do not have their rides with them?" asked Rocky.

The animals looked at each other and said, "That makes sense! If we are not with them, how will they come to us?"

But Ballu was **SUSPICIOUS**. "I think this is a way to disrupt our strike."

Rocky knew the animals would not survive if they were not fed immediately. He thought hard and came up with an idea.

He pointed towards Grandpa and said, "He is Eravat, Lord Indra's vehicle. Your prayers have made Lord Indra happy and he has sent this food with him. But if you do not wish to eat, we will inform King Indra."

Before Rocky could complete his sentence, the animals **JUMPED** at the food and polished it off. They felt stronger after eating.

"We were not aware that we are vehicles of various gods till Pandit Bholaram and Bunty the Monkey told us that. Now we know how **IMPORTANT** we are," said Motu. On hearing Bholaram and Bunty's names, both Grandpa and Rocky were surprised.

"Chuchu, please help me pick up this empty box of sweets and throw it," said Grandpa after a little thought.

Chuchu tried to pick up the box but he couldn't move it.

"Try harder! You claim to carry Lord Ganesha across the **universe** on your back, so this should not be difficult for you," said Grandpa.

Chuchu was embarrassed.

Rocky then asked Motu, "Can you throw this box outside?"

"Where is the box?" asked Motu looking around. "It's day time. I cannot see anything when there is sunlight. Let the sun set. Once it gets dark…" he trailed off.

"What if Goddess Lakshmi has to go somewhere during the day?" asked Rocky. Motu had no answer.

"Pandit Bholaram has **fooled** you! You are not the vehicles of gods and no one will help you succeed if you give money to such pandits. Success can only be achieved with hard work," explained Grandpa.

Meanwhile in the **jungle**, Bholaram and Bunty were busy packing their stuff and getting ready to run away.

Grandpa took all the animals to Bholaram and Bunty's house where they saw the two dividing the money they had been given.

On seeing Grandpa, the two immediately *realised* they had been found out. Before anyone could say anything, they returned all the money they had got from the animals.

Grandpa and Rocky then left for Vijayvan. On the way back, Grandpa **THOUGHT** : "We need to open a school and a library here, so that the residents of Devvan cannot be fooled easily. They need books that will help them think for themselves."

JAGMUG GLOWS AGAIN

By Harendra Chakravarty

"Jagmug, my friend, why do you look so upset?" asked Chatru the Sparrow, looking at Jagmug the Firefly's sad face.

"No one cares for me anymore. Since **tubelights** have been installed in Chandavan, we fireflies have lost our importance," replied Jagmug, pointing towards a street light.

Chatru nodded. Before Chandavan had electricity, fireflies had **LIT UP** ✹ the forest paths. In return, the animals gave the fireflies money and food. But with the introduction of electric lights, the fireflies had no work. Many of them moved to other forests looking for work.

Jagmug did not want to leave his home in Chandavan. He understood the importance of lighting, and took the trouble to learn about **ELECTRICITY** and wiring. He decided to look for a job in Chandavan Electricity Department. He went to Jojo the Jackal, who was in charge of the department.

"Jojo, I would like to work with you," began Jagmug. "I know the lighting needs of Chandavan, and I have also begun studying about **wiring** and electricity."

"Jagmug, your days are over!" said Jojo scornfully.

"Just because you once provided **light** here does not mean you understand anything about the electricity department. We engineers are the best at this job!"

"Why don't you go to another forest like your friends?" asked Jacky the Giraffe, who also worked in the department. They laughed at Jagmug.

WHAT IS JAGMUG'S CUP OF TEA?

"I won't leave Chandavan," **YELLED** Jagmug. "I will go complain to the king when he returns from his meetings abroad. Not one of you has even managed to pass your primary school exams and you call yourselves engineers!"

Jacky and Jojo were furious. They tried chasing Jagmug, but the **firefly** flew among the trees and could not be caught. Jagmug reached the safety of his home and began to get ready for bed when Chatru knocked at the door.

"Jagmug, aren't you coming to the airport to receive the king?" asked   Chatru. "We are all going. You should come too!"

Jagmug was reluctant, but Chatru persuaded him. "You may be able to **speak** with the king about your job problem," said Chatru.

Jagmug agreed, and along with all the other inhabitants of Chandavan, set off to welcome the king.

The airport was crowded, as all the animals and **BiRDS** wanted to greet their king, who had been gone for more than a week. One of the birds spotted the royal Chandavan Airlines aeroplane in the distance, and everyone began to cheer. They knew Baga the Vulture, the pilot, would land the aeroplane right in front of them.

The airport manager ran in to **SWITCH** on the runway lights, so Baga could see where he was to land. But when he flipped the switch, all the lights went out! It was a general electricity failure. Jojo and Jacky brought out all their tools and tried to find the problem. But it was **PITCH DARK,** and all the animals began to feel very afraid. "The plane will run out of fuel very soon, and Baga cannot land in such darkness," said the airport manager. Nobody knew what to do.

In all the confusion, Jagmug **slipped** away and made some phone calls. In a short time, fireflies from the other forests flocked to the Chandavan Airport. Under Jagmug's directions, they flew to the runway and illuminated it. Baga could see clearly now, and landed the plane safely.

The king got off the plane with Baga, and headed straight to the fireflies to thank them. "You saved our lives!" exclaimed Baga. "Now we have to **see** why electricity failed at such a critical time."

Jacky came running up. "Sir, the electricity went off because Jojo insisted on using **POOR** quality cables. You had given him a lot of money for the cables, and he spent only very little. The rest of the money he kept for himself! When I saw what had happened, I was going to bring him to you for punishment, but he ran away!"

The king was FURIOUS. "You and Jojo told me you were engineers! From now on, the electricity department will be handled only by those who understand Chandavan's lighting needs. The fireflies, headed by Jagmug, will be in charge."

The other inhabitants of Chandavan, who had seen how well Jagmug and his friends handled the crisis, cheered loudly, and the proud fireflies glowed even brighter!

Light it up!

Spot 5 fireflies in the picture below.

Answer on the last page

FALSE IMPRESSIONS

By Indrajit Kaushik

"Bow, wow, wow!"

"Every time I walk past, these dogs bark at me!" thought Gajju the Elephant. This time, the dogs did not stop at barking. They **began** to chase Gajju. "Run, Gajju," shouted Peelu the Deer. "Those dogs are going to get you. Run!"

Gajju ran away from the dogs as fast as he could. Ratty the Mouse, sitting on a branch, saw this and laughed. CLAPPING her hands, she shouted: "Look at that! An elephant is running so fast!"

Ratty did not notice that a cat was stalking her, and when she was distracted by Gajju running, the cat POUNCED! Luckily, Ratty moved at the same time, and only a bit of her tail was swiped off by the cat. The cat raced away and Ratty shrieked in pain.

RATU THE RESCUER

Ratty's brother, Ratu, came RUNNING when he heard his sister cry out. "What hurt you, Ratty?" he asked.

"It was that evil elephant, Gajju. He tried to step on me on purpose. Had I moved **slower,** he would surely have trampled me!" cried Ratty.

"How dare he!" yelled Ratu. "That Gajju has made a **HUGE** mistake, picking on you." He rushed away to his office.

"Why did you lie to Ratu?" asked Tarru the Frog. "I saw that it was the cat that took your **tail** off!"

"I don't need to lie to you, Tarru. I am just taking revenge on Gajju. He refused to give me a ride on his back last week!" said Ratty.

Ratu published a daily **newspaper** for the forest. That day, he wrote a piece on how Gajju was frightening all the smaller animals. When the animals read it, they all began avoiding Gajju.

Poor Gajju tried clearing his name, but because they read about him in the newspaper, the animals were unwilling to believe him. They **TRUSTED** the news they read. Gajju was alone, and went deeper into the forest because he had no friends.

The monsoons arrived soon. One day, the **rain** was particularly heavy, and the animals desperately looked for shelter. Some took shelter in caves and burrows on the mountainside, while others took to the trees and hid inside hollows and under branches.

Gajju too was **SEEKING** shelter under a tree when he heard cries for help. It was coming from a rabbit's burrow. The river had flooded, and the water had entered the burrow. Some of the baby rabbits were being **swept** away by the current. Other animals that had taken shelter in the burrows were also being washed away.

Hearing their cries, Gajju raced towards the river. Bigger animals **shouted** to him to stay away. "You'll get washed away, Gajju! Save yourself!" they yelled. Gajju ignored them. He soon reached the water and saw the animals **struggling** to save themselves. He overtook them and stood in front of them. "Quick! Climb on my back and I'll take you to safety!" he trumpeted.

The smaller animals climbed on, and Gajju took them to **HIGHER** ground. Thanks to Gajju's bravery, all the animals were safe.

When it stopped raining, Gajju took the smaller animals back to their families. The entire forest celebrated. The animals **apologised** to Gajju for treating him so badly based on one article in the paper. Ratu also apologised for publishing that story. Gajju accepted the apologies and agreed to come back and live with the other animals.

Then Ratu asked Gajju to apologise to Ratty for **STEPPING** on her tail. Gajju was puzzled. "I didn't step on her tail. In fact, I haven't seen her since that day she was

sitting on a tree laughing at me because I was being chased by two dogs!"

Ratty realised the game was up, and before anyone could ask her anything, she **CONFESSED**. "I only told a lie to take revenge because Gajju didn't give me a ride on his back," she said. "I'm very sorry, Gajju. I promise I will not do something like this again."

Gajju accepted her apology, and life went on **HAPPILY** in the forest.

..........🐌..........

MIRACLE UNDONE

By Isha Agarwal

This year, when Bunty visited his grandmother's village during the summer HOLIDAYS, he noticed that the village lacked its usual buzz. Normally, the place was flooded with activity in the evenings. He asked his friends, Shanky, Jeetu and Manjeet, what was happening.

"A miracle baba is visiting our village these days. The villagers go to seek his blessings," Shanky said.

"How do you know he has MIRACULOUS powers?" Bunty asked.

"Because he sent an idol of God to the heavens with his powers," replied Jeetu.

"But that is not possible," said Bunty.

"You will also start believing once you see Babaji perform a miracle," Manjeet said.

When Bunty went back to his grandmother's house, he asked her about the baba. She said the same thing his friends had told him.

The next day, Grandma took Bunty to take Babaji's blessings.

The baba had settled in the ruins behind a temple, near the lake. Bunty saw him sitting on a throne, surrounded by his disciples. Each and every visitor took babaji's blessings and put money in the **BOX** kept there.

The baba waved his hand in the air and **FLOWERS** appeared out of nowhere. Not only that, he turned a coin into ash, just by muttering a few words. Everybody praised baba for his miracles.

"Last night, God came in my dreams and asked me to send his **idol** to heaven by immersing it in the lake," announced the baba. He then went into the temple, brought out an idol, and immersed it in the lake. While he did this, the villagers continued chanting prayers. Once the idol was immersed, the baba came out of the lake. "Now, go back to your houses. We will send the rest of the idols to heaven on the full moon day."

"Dadi, isn't this idol very old and **precious?**" asked Bunty.

"Yes, but Baba is doing us a favour by sending it to God directly and **blessing** the village."

The villagers went home. Bunty, meanwhile, was **SUSPICIOUS.** He asked his friends to come to the lake after sunset. That night, after Grandma had slept, Bunty and his friends reached the lake.

"Why have you called us here at this time?" Jeetu asked.

Just then, they heard some **NOISES** coming from the temple. Bunty signalled to his friends to remain quiet by putting a finger on his lips. From behind the bushes, where they were hiding, they saw the baba arrive with his disciples.

One of the disciples walked into the lake and brought out the same idol of God that the baba had **CLAIMED** he had sent to heaven in front of the villagers. The baba gave the idol to another disciple and said, "Go and deliver this to our people in the city."

Then he *pulled* out a mobile phone from his robe and dialled a number.

"This is Goga speaking. One of my men will be coming to you with an idol today, I will send the rest of the idols in a couple of days; keep my full payment ready."

"Boss, if we make so many idols *disappear* together, won't the villagers get suspicious?" asked one of the disciples.

"We have been SMUGGLING so many valuable idols for days now, the villagers haven't suspected anything," replied Baba. Hearing this, they all laughed. As soon as they left, Bunty and his friends ran from there and stopped only when they reached the village school.

"Bunty, this baba is a thief," Jeetu said, gasping for breath.

"I had a doubt. That's why I called all of you," Bunty said.

"What are you children doing here?" It was the schoolmaster, who lived just behind the **SCHOOL**🏫. He was surprised to see the children roaming about so late in the evening, and asked them to come to his house and explain.

Bunty told him what had happened.

"I tried explaining to the villagers that they shouldn't believe in such miracle babas, but they did not listen to me," said the schoolmaster.

"What shall we do now?" asked Shanky.

Bunty used the schoolmaster's computer to **search** for the baba. He found that the baba was actually a smuggler and the police in several cities were looking for him. Bunty realised that it was important to expose the baba in front of the villagers. He thought of a plan and quickly told the others.

Two days later, on the full **moon** night when Goga and his men were carrying **ANCIENT** idols from temples towards the lake for immersion, Bunty fell on the ground and started shaking violently.

"Bunty has been possessed by God," screamed Shanky. The villagers were stunned to hear this.

37

Bunty pointed to the baba and his men and said in a **GRUFF** voice, "Today, I will take my devotees with me to heaven; immerse them in the lake with me."

The villagers immediately picked up the baba and his disciples and started walking towards the lake.

The baba and his men were **SCARED** as they knew they would drown in the deep lake if they were immersed.

TRUTH REVEALS

"Let go of us!" Baba screamed.

"But we have to follow God's instructions; let's **immerse** them, friends!" said the villagers.

"Stop it! This is not the path to heaven," Baba cried.

"Then how were you sending our temple idols to **heaven?**" asked the schoolmaster, stepping forward from the crowd.

Baba had no answer to the question. Bunty looked at the villagers and said, "This is no baba. His real name is Goga, who came to our village and changed his identity to steal ancient idols from our village temples."

The villagers were shocked to hear this. "But how did he **perform** all those miracles?" asked the headman.

"He learnt magic tricks, like catching flowers in the air or turning a coin to ash, to fool us," Bunty replied.

The **POLICE** arrived and handcuffed Goga and his men. The inspector pulled the baba's beard to show Goga's face and also showed the villagers the idols that he had stolen. He praised Bunty and said, "Bunty, you have shown great **courage** and intelligence in catching Goga. I will recommend your name for a bravery award."

The villagers congratulated Bunty for his efforts. "I could not have done this alone. My friends and the schoolmaster were equally important," said Bunty. His friends hugged him for that. When the holidays were over and Bunty had to return home, the entire village came to see him off. After all, he had saved them from a miracle baba!

PUZZLE TIME

MATCH THE COLUMN

In Column B, Babaji and his men have disguised themselves. Match the man in Column A with his disguised look.

COLUMN A

COLUMN B

Answer on the last page

JENNY-KATHY'S FLYING MACHINE

By Richa Chhapolika

"**D**idi, when will we be able to fly in the **SKY?**" Kathy the Tortoise asked her sister, Jenny.

"Kathy, we cannot **fly** because nature has created us to swim in water or live on land," explained Jenny.

"But humans who live on land don't have **WINGS.** They are able to fly in their flying machines. So why can't we?" asked Kathy.

Baggu the Heron was standing nearby and **listening** 👂 to their conversation. He laughed at Kathy. "Some people have their feet on the land, but dream of the sky," he said. Kathy felt bad being **laughed** 😆 at, but was determined to find a way to fly with Jenny on a flying machine.

She kept thinking about this day and night. But she could not think of a way to fly.

One day, she was sitting by the *riverside* looking up at the sky. Suddenly, a toy aeroplane fell down near her. Frightened, she ran to hide behind a rock. Nothing happened, so she peeped out and then crept up to the toy.

DON'T HIDE TO DISCOVER

"Oh, this is indeed a flying machine!" she exclaimed and ran to call her sister.

"Didi, come **QUICKLY**! I want to show you something!" she called.

"What is it, Kathy? I've got a lot of work to do. Can't this wait?" asked Jenny.

"No, Didi. It's urgent. Please come now!"

"Oh, alright! Let's go," said Jenny, and followed Kathy.

Kathy dragged her sister to the spot where the toy plane had fallen, but there was nothing to be found. "Where has it gone? It was right here!" **exclaimed** Kathy, shocked that she was not able to find the plane.

"What is it, Kathy?" asked Jenny.

Kathy explained.

"It must have been a **toy** aeroplane," explained Jenny. "A child must have been playing, and would have come and **PiCKED** it up by the time you brought me here. Don't cry, Kathy!"

"Didi, I want a flying machine!" sobbed Kathy.

Jenny couldn't stop Kathy from crying. She thought of how she could get a flying machine and suddenly had an **IDEA**. She could make a toy plane, just like the humans did!

"Kathy, I promise you will get your flying machine," said Jenny confidently.

"How, Didi? Tell me," asked Kathy, **drying** her tears.

"We'll make one!" announced Jenny.

"Is it possible?" asked Kathy, hopefully.

"Everything is POSSIBLE if one tries," Jenny said lovingly.

The two started working on their flying machine. Kathy found a picture of a flying machine, and with the help of the river creatures, they collected wood, motor, **BATTERY**, tyres, clips, wires, plastic, glue, and everything else they could need.

They took two wooden boards and fitted the motor in the centre. Then they glued on more boards to create the skeleton of the aeroplane and then added the wings and tail. They then connected the battery to the motor. Wheels, seats, steering, and **DOORS** and windows were then added with the help of their river friends. Finally, Jenny whispered something to Kathy, and they made a large wooden box with big glass walls and fitted that below the body of the aeroplane. Finally, they covered everything in bright plastic sheets and the plane was ready!

"Hurray! Our flying machine is ready!" cried Kathy, **jumping** with excitement.

"Congratulations, Jenny and Kathy!" said Crabby the Crab. "I'm so proud that you've done this!"

"I'm so **HAPPY** for you both," chimed in Maya the Fish.

"Why don't you fly this now?" asked Inky the Octopus.

"Yes, of course! Kathy, are you ready to go up in the sky?" asked Jenny, holding on to Kathy.

"Let's go, Didi," shouted Kathy, and the two **climbed** in. They started the plane, and very soon, they were up in the sky!

"I can't **believe** we are actually flying!" exclaimed Kathy.

"Everything is possible if you work towards it," said Jenny, smiling at her sister.

They decided to land near the river, and climbed down from the **PLANE**. They only saw sad faces when they came down.

"What's the matter? Why are you all looking so sad?" Kathy asked Crabby.

"We too would **LOVE** to fly with you, but we are water creatures and cannot leave the river," said Inky sadly.

Jenny had run back to the plane and opened the wooden box she and Kathy had fitted in. Meanwhile, Kathy **SMILED** at her river friends. "Didi says everything is possible if we work for it!"

"But flying is not possible for us. We cannot survive outside the water," said Maya.

"Come, look!" said Kathy and Jenny. The water creatures swam up to the plane and saw the big box filled with water. "**Swim** in, friends!" exclaimed Jenny. "We can all fly now," said Kathy laughing with excitement.

The tortoise sisters climbed into the plane, their aquatic friends swam into the box below, and soon they were all flying up in the sky.

Baggu was flying by. "What is happening? Am I *dreaming?* Tortoise, fish, crab, and octopus are flying in the sky! How is this possible?" He tumbled down in shock.

This time it was Kathy's turn to laugh at Baggu.

THE FLYING RABBIT

By Renu Mandal

Terry the Rabbit was very upset. "These sparrows are so lucky. How I wish I could fly like them! They can fly everywhere. They don't even have to walk to school like me. I become tired by the time I reach school. I wish I could get wings so that I can fly."

TERRY WANTS TO FLY

One day, Terry was playing on the river bank when he found two pigeon feathers. He was **DELIGHTED** and carried them home carefully. At home, he used glue to stick the feathers to his back and then walked out into the garden.

Daisy the Sparrow was sitting on the branch of a mango tree, and Terry ran up to her. "Daisy, now I can fly just like you."

"Really? How can you do that?" asked Daisy.

Terry climbed the tree and **jumped** off the branch, trying to flutter the pigeon feathers. He fell to the ground with a **THUD**. "Terry, you can't fly just by attaching two *feathers* to your back," said Daisy, laughing hard.

Terry got up and **DUSTED**

himself off. "Let's bet on this. What will you give me if I start flying within a month?"

"Oh, forget it!" said Daisy. "There's no way you can win that bet!"

"I'll definitely fly within a month," said Terry confidently.

"Well, if you do that, I'll be your servant for a month," said Daisy with a grin.

Terry agreed and walked home **thoughtfully**. He spent a sleepless night thinking of how he could start flying. He couldn't come up with a solution despite thinking all night.

TERRY GOT INSPIRED

The next day, Terry had to go to school. His science teacher, Sammy the Deer, was talking about the 18th century, when **balloons** were filled with hot air and used as flying machines. He also mentioned the Wright brothers, who built the first aeroplane.

Terry was inspired by the **idea** of using balloons to fly. After school, he ran to the market and bought a huge transparent balloon and got it filled with helium. The **MOMENT** it was filled, the balloon **rose** up in the air. Terry quickly tied the mouth of the balloon with a long piece of string and held on to the other end of the string. As the balloon rose, it took Terry up into the *air.*

The transparent balloon couldn't be seen easily, and all the birds thought Terry was flying! Daisy and her friends **flew** up to Terry to make sure he was indeed flying. "You've won the bet," Daisy said. "Now you can go back down!"

Terry didn't want to land when the birds could see him, because he knew they would see the balloon and realise that he wasn't really flying. Also, he was thoroughly **ENJOYING** the experience of flying higher and higher! But after a while, the gas started leaking out of the **BALLOON**, and as it deflated, it could no longer hold Terry up and the little rabbit soon fell to the ground with a thud.

All the birds saw that Terry had been flying with the help of a balloon and began to **laugh** at him. Daisy **HOPPED** up to where Terry was lying on the ground. "You deserve these injuries for pretending you could fly!" she exclaimed.

Teacher Sammy came out hearing the noise. When he understood what had happened, he said: "Terry, **nature** has made every animal unique. Birds cannot run and jump like us, and we cannot fly like them. It is foolish to imitate anyone. Now let me take you to a doctor because you fell to the ground pretty hard!"

Terry understood what his teacher was saying, and before being taken to the doctor, he apologised to Daisy for trying to cheat. "I guess I'll stay a rabbit and you stay a bird!" he said.

FLY  AWAY!

Identify which objects will fly if the fan is switched on.

Answer on the last page

SMART MICE

By Vivek Chakravarty

Sonu stood staring at the piece of **CAKE** on the floor. As he was standing there, two tiny mice came to eat it. Sonu clapped his hands loudly, and the mice scampered away. He began laughing at this.

Hearing the **laughter**, Sonu's younger brother Monu came running in. "What happened, brother? Why are you laughing?"

MICE FAIL

"Two mice came in to eat this piece of cake," explained Sonu. "I **clapped** my hands and they were so scared! It was quite funny to see them run away."

"Oh, I would also **LOVE** to see this!" exclaimed Monu. "Where are the mice? Let's scare them again!"

"They are hiding," explained Sonu. "Come and sit quietly on the cot with me and let's wait."

The two boys sat on the bed. Suddenly, Sonu got up. "I've got an even better idea!" he said. He picked up the piece of cake and tied it with a **string** and hung it several inches above the ground. "Now let's see what happens!" he said and got up on the bed again.

INVESTIGATING THE CASE OF THE MISSING CAKE

The two boys waited quietly. Sure enough, after a while, a mouse peeped out. Seeing the coast clear, it ran to the cake, but however hard it tried, it couldn't reach it. It tried **jumping**, and even tried standing on two legs, but it tumbled over and fell. Sonu and Monu could no longer control themselves and **burst** out laughing. The mouse scurried away.

"Let's sit quietly and see if another mouse comes out!" said Monu. So they waited again, and another mouse came out. It tried to reach the cake, but it also fell down. This happened a few times, and the boys were thoroughly **ENTERTAINED.**

"Isn't it wonderful to trouble mice, which otherwise only trouble us?" asked Sonu. "Am I not the smartest person to have thought of something like this?"

Monu agreed with these **BOASTFUL** claims, and the boys soon had to get ready for bed.

"What shall we do with the cake?" asked Monu.

"Leave it. Let the mice try to get it all **night!**" was Sonu's reply.

The boys soon fell asleep. The next morning, they woke up and found the cake **gone!**

"How did the cake vanish?" demanded Sonu.

"Mum or Dad must have thrown it away," suggested Monu. But Sonu shook his head. "If they did that, they would have thrown away the string also. But look, the string is there. Only the cake has gone. I think the mice managed to get it!"

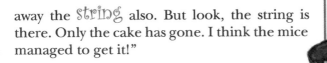

"But how could they, Sonu?" asked Monu. "They could barely **reach** it yesterday."

"The only way to find out is by repeating the experiment," announced Sonu.

He got another piece of cake, and **tied** it up exactly as he had done the day before.

The two boys sat *silently* on the bed and waited.

Pretty soon, a mouse scampered up. It tried jumping for the cake, and even tried standing on its hind legs, but could not reach the cake.

"This happened yesterday also," **whispered** Monu.

"Shhh!" said Sonu. "Let us see what happens."

The mouse was still trying to get the cake by standing on two legs, when another mouse joined it. But instead of jumping, the second mouse **stood** on the shoulders of the first mouse and easily got the cake. The two mice carried the piece of cake away.

"I never thought mice could be so *clever*," gasped Sonu.

"I've learnt two things from this," said Monu.

"What is that?" asked Sonu.

"One, that there is strength in unity. When the mice tried to get the cake separately, they failed. But when they worked together, they got the cake easily!"

"You're right, Monu. And what is the second thing?" asked Sonu.

"The second is that we should never underestimate anyone or anything. We are not the cleverest creatures in the world!"

Sonu agreed. The mice had taught him a LESSON he would never forget.

THE WORLD OF HOOLOCK GiBBONS

By Kumud Kumar

Jumpy the Monkey loved to travel. His trips had taken him to many parts of India. He had now decided to tour the North East. He booked a **TICKET** to Guwahati, the biggest city of Assam. After travelling around the city, Jumpy headed off to explore the **JUNGLES** of Assam.

JUMPY'S TOUR OF THE JUNGLE

As he roamed through the dense forest, he came across a hoolock gibbon. Both became friends. At **SUNSET**, the gibbon took Jumpy home and offered him fruits to eat. As they relaxed, Jumpy wanted to know more about his new friend.

Munching on a banana, the gibbon began: "You and I both belong to the **PRIMATE** family, Jumpy. But you belong to the monkey category, while I belong to the ape category. Apes include gorillas, chimpanzees, gibbons, and orangutans."

"What is the difference between monkeys and apes?" asked Jumpy.

"Well, you can see the physical differences between us," said the gibbon. "Apes like me can **swing** from tree to tree using our arms. You monkeys have long tails and a different shoulder structure and you jump from branch to branch, don't you?"

"Yes! We do jump a lot. That's why I'm called Jumpy!" The gibbon laughed with Jumpy at this.

"But are you very different from humans?" asked Jumpy *CURIOUSLY*.

"I'm sure you asked me that because my face resembles a human face," said the gibbon. Jumpy nodded. "Well, the big difference is in how our limbs are shaped. Human hands and legs are shaped very differently, whereas those of apes are quite similar. Our legs can do the same work as our hands."

MEETING A WELL-INFORMED GUIDE

Jumpy was **fascinated** by his new friend, who was like him in some ways and totally unlike him in others. "Tell me more about apes," he asked.

"Well, gorillas and chimpanzees are mainly found in Africa. Orangutans are mainly to be found on the **islands** of Sumatra and Borneo. Gibbons like me are found exclusively in Asia. You will find us in the jungles of Malaysia and, of course, Assam!"

"Do you look different from the gibbons in

Malaysia?" Jumpy wanted to know.

"There's not much of a difference. The apes found in Assam have white eyebrows, whereas Malaysian apes have white hands," said his friend. "Oh, and I must tell you that we are the **SHORTEST** in the whole ape family! As you see, I'm around two feet tall. We gibbons like to live in large groups in dense but rocky mountains. The human locals here call us Tukku."

"Tell me more," begged Jumpy, wanting to learn everything he could about his new friend.

"The male gibbon is brownish black like me, with this white slanted streak on the eyebrows. The female gibbon is almost **fully** brown. Our colonies usually have 80 to 100 gibbons. We spend most of our time on trees, but climb down to search for food. That is when we walk on our feet like humans, but we cannot run too fast."

"What do you do every day? I mean, what's your routine?" asked Jumpy.

"Well, Jumpy, you may find our chattering loud and harsh, but that's how we make our presence felt in the jungle. We start chattering around **DAWN** and go on till past 9 a.m. Then we stop because it's time to search for food. We look for **food**, eat, and rest till dusk, when we return to our colonies and start chattering again!"

"Do you care for your babies like we do?" was Jumpy's next question.

"Yes, Jumpy. We take special CARE of our young ones. Our females give birth to a single YOUNG one at a time. A mother gibbon holds her baby close to her body for almost 7 months."

"What do you usually eat?" asked Jumpy.

"Our diet is pretty similar to yours," said the gibbon. "We eat fruits and flowers. We also eat some small insects, ants, eggs, and even some tiny birds sometimes. We are fond of spiders. Our habit of drinking water is similar to that of monkeys."

"Brother gibbon, from all you have told me, I find that your species has may similarities to both humans and monkeys!" Jumpy and the gibbon shared a laugh at this, and then got ready for bed.

Jumpy was happy that he had met a new friend and learnt so much from him. "I should next go to the jungles of Malaysia and meet this gibbon's cousins!" he thought sleepily, as the MOON rose over the Assam forest.

ACHAL'S CURIOSITY

By Ilika Priy

Once, a tremor shook the Earth and a little mountain was born. He looked around and found himself surrounded by huge mountains.

"Who are you?" asked the little **MOUNTAIN**.

One big mountain replied, "We are the neighbours of the mighty Himalayas."

"Who am I?" asked the little mountain.

The **big** mountain was puzzled. He thought for a while and said, "Well, till now, humans have given us our names. From today onwards, I will call you Achal." The little mountain was happy.

As days passed, small plants began to grow on him. When Achal looked at the big mountain, he saw that there were no plants on him. Achal asked, "Uncle, why are these plants growing on me and not on you?"

The big mountain replied, "That's because I am more than 16,000 feet **TALL** and you are shorter than 12,000 feet.

CURIOSITY LEADS TO INFORMATION

"What does that mean?" Achal asked.

The big mountain replied, "Plants grow easily up to a height of 12,000 feet. Above 14,000 feet only bushes **survive** and above 16,000 feet even grass cannot survive."

Achal was curious. "Why is that?"

"As the altitude increases, there are changes in our atmosphere; there is less oxygen and a decline in temperature. Plants need **oxygen** and **WARMTH** to grow," explained the big mountain. Achal was satisfied.

It was summer; the ice on the top of the big mountain was melting slowly. Achal asked the mountain about it.

"I am a glacier and my **ice** melts into water whereas you are a rock mountain."

One day, Achal saw a group of people. "Who are those people *walking* up on me? Where are they from?" he asked the big mountain.

"Oh! They are trekkers," said the big mountain.

TREKKING IS A NICE HOBBY

"What is trekking?"

"It is a hobby. Trekkers climb on mountains, live on us for days and study the weather. They **calculate** ⊞ our height, study the animals and plants that live on us

and also conduct a few other activities."

Achal still looked at them with suspicion. Suddenly, the cylinder on a trekker's back caught his **attention**. He asked, "Uncle, what's that?"

"That's a gas cylinder. As altitude increases, oxygen level decreases, causing headache, nausea and tiredness. Therefore, they carry oxygen cylinders and use them when required," explained the big mountain.

Achal was calm for a **LITTLE** while. Suddenly, he looked down and shouted again in amazement, "Now, what is that?"

"Don't **shout!** He is taking out a water bottle. The air is dry here, so they need fluid at regular intervals or else they will get dehydrated. During trekking, one should drink 3 to 4 litres of water every day."

"What do you mean every day? For how many days are they going to stay here?" Achal questioned again.

"They cannot climb up and come down in one day. If they reach our peak directly, they will get ill. They need to **rest** after climbing every 2,000 feet."

The big mountain added: "They rest during the night and are ready to climb further the next day. If they trek at **HIGH** altitudes, they have to be very careful. The usual and safe practice is to trek up to about 2,000 feet and to camp at a lower altitude. The next day, they climb higher, but again come down a few hundred feet to **camp** . They do this so that their body can adjust or acclimatise to the low oxygen levels. They find the path with the least depressions and **CRACKS**, where there is less danger. If required, they use ropes to climb up."

"Do we face any problem because of them?" Achal asked.

"No, we don't face any **PrOBLeM**. They come here every year," the big mountain said.

Achal was **HAPPY** as all his questions were answered. If a new mountain came up beside him, he knew he would be able to help it with information too.

BiNNi'S TRiP

By Vivek Chakravarty

T̲he Shatabdi Express coming from Delhi stopped at the Charbagh station of Lucknow. Even before the train **stopped**, Porter Chuchu the Mouse ran to the AC compartment.

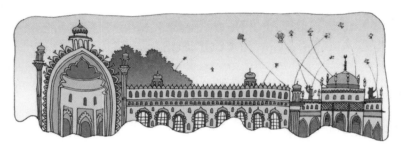

"Welcome to the City of Nawabs," said Chuchu sensing someone coming towards the door.

"Porter, take my luggage to the auto stand."

"Yes, madam!" said Chuchu lifting the suitcase, and then turning to the passenger.

"A cat!" screamed Chuchu and dropped the **suitcase** and fled.

"I had heard that Lucknow is the city of 𝓇𝒾𝒸𝒽 culture and respect. What kind of respect is this that allows you to throw someone's suitcase and flee? Thankfully my suitcase is a good brand, or else it would have broken," cried Binni Cat.

An **ANGRY** Binni lifted her suitcase and walked out of the railway station.

She hired an autorickshaw to the hotel she had found in Hazratganj. Once she was in her room, she rested for a while and then decided to go see the city. She **hired** a taxi, and after driving past some of Lucknow's famous monuments such as Rumi Darwaza, she reached the Chota Imambara.

"If I hire a guide, I'll have to spend money. It is better that I quietly follow a group of **tourists** who have a guide. I will listen to the guide and get to know more about the places without paying any money," thought Binni. She found a group of tourists and started following it.

BECOME FRIENDS WITH STRANGERS

"The main building of the Imambara is right in front, but these people are walking towards the left. **STRANGE!** Maybe there is another famous place there, which I am not aware of," thought Binni, following the group.

The group headed to a playground where a number of people were *flying* kites. The group joined them.

An annoyed Binni decided to hire a guide who took her through Chota Imambara. "Madam, this is it. Please pay my fee of ₹500," said the guide at the end of the TOUR.

"But you haven't yet taken me around Bada Imambara!" said Binni.

"Madam, I'm a guide only for this place," said the guide, "Bada Imambara is a **different** area and you would need to hire another guide for touring that place."

"Which means I'll have to spend more money," said Binni angrily, handing over the money. She then left for Bada Imambara.

She began **searching** 🔍 for a guide there. She was feeling hot and sweaty. She wiped her face, took a folding fan from her bag and began fanning herself.

"Madam, do you need a guide to tour Bada Imambara and the Bhool Bhulaiya?" someone asked and Binni turned towards him.

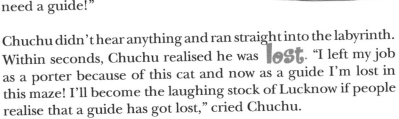

"A cat!" screamed Chuchu, **running** 🐁 away as fast as possible.

"Please wait," called Binni. "I really need a guide!"

Chuchu didn't hear anything and ran straight into the labyrinth. Within seconds, Chuchu realised he was **lost**. "I left my job as a porter because of this cat and now as a guide I'm lost in this maze! I'll become the laughing stock of Lucknow if people realise that a guide has got lost," cried Chuchu.

Just then, he saw a group of tourists walking around and followed them. Pretty soon, Chuchu was out of the maze. He had never felt so relieved!

"I think I'll become a taxi driver," thought Chuchu. "It's too risky being a porter or a guide!"

CAT IN THE TAXI!

The next day, Chuchu was in a taxi, waiting for tourists outside the Lucknow Residency. Tourists were entering other taxis, but he had no passengers. Suddenly, the back door of his taxi opened and someone entered. "Drive me to the Residency!" commanded a voice.

Chuchu turned around in **SURPRISE** because he was at the entrance of the Residency. "Is this a joke?" he began, and then saw who his passenger was. Yes, it was Binni again!

"Why do you keep following me?" squeaked Chuchu as he **scrambled** out of the car to run away.

"I don't do it on purpose. I want to go to see the Residency and you are also running towards it. It isn't my fault!" called out Binni, as she too walked towards the Residency.

Chuchu, meanwhile, hid inside an ancient cannon, and waited for Binni to leave. But Binni began walking towards that same cannon! "This looks so **dramatic!**" exclaimed Binni. "I feel like a soldier and want to fire this," she added, walking closer to the cannon.

Chuchu heard this and jumped out of the cannon and ran helter-skelter to look for a new **HIDING** place. He decided to hide behind a tree in the Residency. "The Residency was where the Indians fought for freedom from the British in 1857," he thought. "Today, I have to fight for my **freedom** from this cat!"

Chuchu peeped out from behind the tree to check if the coast was clear. But there was Binni, busy clicking photos of the Residency from all **ANGLES**. Chuchu sighed and looked up and noticed a boulder rolling down the slope, heading for Binni!

Chuchu **raced** from behind the tree and shoved Binni away from the boulder's path. "Help! My camera! Who pushed me?" yelled Binni, shaken and upset.

"Madam, never mind your **camera**. You would have been squashed by that boulder!" exclaimed Chuchu.

Binni looked around and saw the **boulder** rolling past. "Thank you, you brave mouse! You saved my life! But you have been running away from me all this time. Why did you do this?" asked Binni.

"You are our guest, madam," said Chuchu **PROUDLY**. "As Lucknow residents, we do not want any of our guests hurt."

Then he added quickly: "But you are also a cat, and cats are enemies of mice, so I'll **RUN** away now," and rushed off to hide.

Binni laughed, and continued her tour of Lucknow. But wherever she went, whether it was Kukrail, the clock tower, or the zoo, she managed to run into Chuchu, who still scampered away on **seeing** her.

After a day of trying to hide from the cat, Chuchu reached his taxi again. "I hardly drove this," he said to himself. "Maybe I should give up being a taxi driver and think of another job!"

SURPRISES IN LIFE!

As he reached his cab, he noticed a **mobile** phone and a note on the bonnet of his car. He picked up the note: "Thank you for saving my life at the Residency. This is a small **GIFT** from me to you. I am not your enemy. Your friend, Binni the Cat from Delhi."

Chuchu was thrilled with the latest model of the phone that he had been given. He put it carefully into the taxi, and got in to drive off. "I misjudged that cat," he thought. Suddenly, he heard a **mewing** noise. "Oh no! There's a cat in my car. What shall I do?" thought poor Chuchu.

That's when he noticed that the new phone had **LIT UP**. "Oh, that's the ringtone!" he thought, relieved. "But who knows this new number?" Saying that, he answered the phone.

"Hello!" said a voice. It was Binni. "I just wanted to make sure you got my gift. I won't talk to you for too long now. Bye!"

Before Chuchu could say hello or goodbye, Binni had **DISCONNECTED** the call.

Chuchu laughed to himself. "This cat has proved to me that all cats are not enemies of mice!"

·········· ❧ ··········

PUZZLE TIME

✏ Write a postcard

Binni took a trip to Kerala and saw the tall and beautiful coconut trees. She also went kayaking in the backwaters. She wants to write a postcard to Chuchu, describing her experience. Help her write it.

KABADDi KABADDi

By Vivek Chakravarty

"**W**ith only a minute to go, Team Harivan is leading by 3 points," shouted the commentator. "This is the closest-fought kabaddi match we have **seen** in a long time. Team Sundervan needs 4 points if it wants to win!"

The inter-forest kabaddi match had everyone tense. "Team Harivan players have caught the Sundervan raider! What a bold move!" **YELLED** the commentator. "And Team Harivan has entered the finals with that!"

Team Harivan was **ECSTATIC.** "Hurray! If we continue like this, we will win the finals too!" exclaimed Gracy the Rabbit, the Team Harivan captain.

"We won't stand a chance if Team Kandyvan enters the finals," warned Marty the Mouse. "That team has the best kabaddi players we have ever seen!"

"Hey, Marty! Let's **FOCUS** on our own game," said Jojo the Monkey. "We also have great players. That's why we've entered the finals!"

"Have you seen Ellie the Elephant play?" **demanded** Marty.

"She is the best raider I have ever seen. Nobody can defeat any team she is on!"

NEVER LOSE HOPE

"Oh no! We totally forgot about Ellie," said Browny the Bear.

"Don't lose hope," encouraged Gracy. "We are very strong, and if we play well, we can defeat anyone!" She was also WORRIED about Ellie, but did not want her team to feel dejected.

"Well, I hope Kandyvan doesn't enter the finals at all!" said Marty.

"Let's go to our rooms and rest before we PRACTISE for the finals," said Gracy. "Let us not worry about who we will be playing against."

That evening, Gracy called the team together. "I went to watch the other semi-finals," she told them. "Kandyvan defeated Chandanvan by 50 points, and are now in the finals!"

"How can anyone defeat a team with so many points?" demanded Browny, shocked.

"It was Ellie," said Gracy. "She RAIDED Team Chandanvan, and when they tried to catch her, she dragged the entire team to her side of the court. That means she managed to tag the entire opposition team! It was a stunning defeat for Chandanvan, and it was all because of Ellie."

"Ellie!" exclaimed the Harivan team in despair.

"We should go back," said Marty.

"Go back where?" **demanded** the team.

"Go back home, of course! There's no chance of us **winning** the finals with Ellie on their side," said a dejected Marty.

"Marty, we cannot lose hope now. We have made it to the finals and we can't give up now," said Gracy. "I have a game plan for our match. But it all depends on you, Marty."

"What do I have to do?" asked Marty **nervously.**

Gracy explained her plan. "Is that a game plan or a plan to get me killed?" demanded Marty. "That **sounds** very dangerous!"

"Marty, you are small and fast. Only you can help us **SCORE**. If you can do this, we stand a very good chance of winning the title!" said Gracy.

"Yes, Marty. You are the *FASTEST* in the team. You can do this," encouraged Browny.

The team got together to convince Marty, who finally agreed.

The next day, Team Harivan **FACED** Team Kandyvan for the toss. Harivan won and decided to raid first. "Marty, remember what you have to do," whispered Gracy.

"Yes, I'll go to the opposing side and run back as fast as I can," Marty whispered back.

"Don't just run back. Remember to tag as many of their players as **possible**. It will be great if you can tag Ellie!" said Gracy.

The match began. Ellie glared at the Harivan team, and Marty was very scared. But with his team shouting support, he ran towards the opponent's court. Ellie reached out to catch Marty, and almost got him. But Marty *slipped* between her legs and reached the other players.

"Ah, there's a nice mouse!" exclaimed Bunty the Cat, one of the Kandyvan players. "Come here, mouse. I'd like a mid-game snack." **TERRIFIED** of Bunty than he was of Ellie, Marty raced back blindly to his team. In his terror, he bumped into three Kandyvan players, including Ellie.

"Hurray! Marty has **tagged** Ellie!" cried the Harivan team.

MARTY'S COURAGE LEADS TO WIN THE MATCH

The game began to get tense. It was Kandyvan's turn to raid, and Bunty raced across, **hoping** to tag Marty. But Browny and the other players tackled him, leaving Marty to hide behind the others. The Kandyvan team then sent Ellie to raid, but the Harivan team had their **strategy** in place. They avoided tackling her, and ran away to save being tagged. Ellie found that her brute tactics, which had won so many matches, were not working against Harivan. Her poor performance demotivated Team Kandyvan. Harivan players, meanwhile, played even better, and soon **WON** the match with a decisive score of 32 against Kandyvan's 17.

"Hurray! We won!" cried the entire team, **hugging** each other and jumping with joy.

"We played a great game. But let us not forget that we won because of Marty's **COURAGE** at the beginning of the match!" exclaimed Gracy.

Marty jumped up and down with his team. Then he saw Bunty staring at him from across the court, and quickly hid behind Browny. He may have won the match, but he was not going to get into **trouble** with a cat!

THE BOY WHO LOVES MURUKKU

By Lekshmi Gopinathan

Hassan is seven years old. He loves sitting on the shikara, a wooden boat, as Abba rows it through the **beautiful** Dal Lake in Srinagar, Kashmir. It's autumn and the breeze is cool but not cold. But there is a silence in Srinagar, something Hassan isn't used to.

The city has been deserted for a month, and there are **soldiers** everywhere. People are not able to go out freely any more.

As the shikara sails round the lake, Hassan hears a rumbling. It's his tummy, longing for some food! Hassan looks hopefully at Abba, but his father is too busy trying to find even a single tourist who will pay him. No **tourists** means no money.

HASSAN'S DAYDREAM OF MURUKKU

Hassan isn't thinking of money, though. His mind is full of images of food. The round flowers in the pots on some shikaras reminds him of pooris. He can almost taste the *sweet* crumbly roth, the cardamom-scented butter cookies that his mother used to make before this trouble happened. He can see the

sugar crystals sprinkled on the cookies and can smell the **BUTTER**. Perhaps Ammi will make them soon, he thinks. Or maybe she can make that other delightful food, his new favourite crunchy savoury snack.

Hassan looks into the distance, remembering the time he ate that **wonderful** food.

It was summer and the season was good. Abba was rowing a family around Dal Lake, and Hassan was helping him. He could not understand what the family said; they spoke a language he was not familiar with. What he knew was that the two kids – twins – were *extremely* naughty! They were pulling each other's hair and fighting. "Subbu. Srini. Sit down and don't rock the shikara. Remember, this is your last ride before we catch our flight home," the mother had scolded the boys.

"Amma, it's Srini. I didn't do anything. And why is this our last shikara ride?" one of the twins **DEMANDED**.

"I'll explain later. Here, eat some snacks," the mother said, holding out a bag to the twins. They opened the bag, and Hassan smelled something *delicious*. It was an unfamiliar smell, but it made his mouth water. The twins picked out something brown and circular, and one of them bit into it. Hassan could hear the **CRUNCH** of whatever it was. His stomach rumbled.

Just then, the other twin snatched the snack from his brother, and in the scuffle, one fell over the side of the shikara! There was dead silence on the shikara. In the most **heroic** moment of his life, Hassan leapt to the side and held on to the child's wrist.

HASSAN'S INSIDE WORLD

The silence was broken by screams. Abba left the oars and raced to help. Within seconds, Srini was pulled back into the **BOAT** and everyone was delighted. The mother pulled a shaken Srini and scared Subbu into a tight hug.

With a grateful **smile** and tears of relief, she turned to Hassan, "Thank you so much, son. Here, have some murukku," she said, thrusting the bag at Hassan.

With a shy smile, Hassan picked one, biting into it. Instantly, his mouth was filled with the taste of roasted rice, spluttering cumin, and dainty sesame seeds. He looked down at the remaining crescent in his hand. This **tasted** even better than roth, his favourite snack till now.

"Would you like some more murukku?" Subbu asked Hassan, who nodded because his mouth was too full to speak.

That evening, Hassan rushed home and told his Ammi about this wonderful new snack. He was **AFRAID** she would not know of it, and wouldn't be able to make it for him. But she did know about it, and she made them for him. How delicious they had been!

"Hassan!" Abba's loud **voice** pulls him out of his dreams. "What are you dreaming of, son? I've been calling you so many times! Tie the shikara up now."

They slot the shikara into its spot at the boarding point and walk home. Some of Abba's friends and other shikara owners join them and there's a lot of talk about an "article". The adults all seem **worried**. Hassan knows about articles and nouns and prepositions, but doesn't understand why this scares the elders so much.

Hassan leaves the men behind and races home. He sits on the front step, waiting for Ammi. He wishes Abba had not forbidden him from lighting the FIREWORKS left over from the Eid celebrations. But then he starts thinking of murukkus again. Perhaps Ammi will make some for him this evening when she gets home.

"Hassan, your school will remain shut this week, too. You have to stay at home. No going outside and playing," says Abba **sternly**.

"But where is Ammi?" asks Hassan.

"The phones are still not working, so I haven't been able to reach her. I'm going now to look for her. Stay at home, Hassan. That's an order," snaps Abba. "I do hope she is **safe**," he mumbles, but Hassan doesn't hear that. He doesn't notice his father's bleak eyes either. All he's thinking of are the murukkus he will get Ammi to make once she gets home.

...........🦋...........

DAMRU LEARNS HIS LESSONS

By Shantha Nagarajan

"**D**amru, I'll never take you to a party again. Everybody was laughing at you. I'm so ashamed," **shouted** his mother, Bekku the Donkey. She had just returned from a party where Damru had **gobbled** up all the food before anybody could even sit at the table.

"You are very badly behaved," scolded Bekku. "How many times have I told you that it's bad manners to **snatch** food before you are served? And the way you gobble! I have told you so many times how important it is to chew!"

Damru wasn't listening. His **stomach** was hurting because of all the food he had eaten in such a hurry, so he went to bed.

The next day was a school **holiday**. Instead of waiting for his mother to finish cooking, Damru raced off to Gokul the Rabbit's snack shop.

"I'm so tired of boring home food. What's today's special?" he asked Gokul.

"Paper dosa, your favourite," **announced** Gokul, placing the dosa in front of Damru. Even before Gokul removed his hands from the plate, Damru had gobbled up the dosa.

"Aaah!" he screamed. "There's something sticking inside my throat!"

He ran outside, looking for help and saw a large sign that said 'Wily the Wolf's Clinic'. Damru rushed in. Wily and his assistant Chirpy the Sparrow were snoring at their tables.

"Doctor, doctor," brayed Damru. "Something is **STUCK** in my throat. It hurts so much!"

Wily yawned, **grumbled**, and then slowly got up. He stretched, and then said: "Something in your throat? Chirpy, peck it out!" and went back to sleep.

Chirpy flew into Damru's mouth and started pecking at his throat.

"Aaaah! That hurts even more! Stop it!" **SCREAMED** Damru and ran away from the clinic.

He realised that he was close to Dr Jumbo the Elephant's hospital, so he ran there.

Dr Jumbo made Damru sit down and spoke calmly. "So a paper dosa is stuck in your throat?" asked the doctor. "Let me see. Open your mouth **wide** please."

Damru opened his mouth, and Dr Jumbo put his **trunk** in. Pretty soon, he removed something and Damru immediately felt better.

"You seem to have swallowed a stick along with the dosa, Damru," said Dr Jumbo.

DAMRU LEARNS TO CHEW

"Thank you, Doctor! I feel so much better," said a relieved Damru. "That Wily is a fraud, but I hoped he could help. But he made me **feel** worse! I think I'll go home now," said Damru, heading for the door.

"Stop right there!" **EXCLAiMED** the doctor. "Come back and sit here, Damru."

Damru nervously went back.

"I will not let you leave till you learn two things," said Jumbo. "The first is what I know your mother has been telling you for many years. Chew your food **carefully** before you swallow! Don't gobble your food. If you do, you may end up with more sticks in your throat!"

"Yes, doctor. I will never gobble my food again," *promised* Damru.

"That's not all. The second lesson you have to learn is to see a **QUALIFIED** doctor in case you don't feel well. Those two unqualified animals could have killed you because they have no understanding of medicine!"

Damru nodded. He had learnt his lessons painfully. He went straight home, and **surprised** his mother by waiting to be served, and then by slowly chewing and enjoying the **DELICIOUS** pakoras she had made.

MAGIC VERSUS LOGIC

By Harbans Singh

Aabha was **thrilled** because her school had declared a holiday due to heavy rains. She wanted to go to the market near her house, but her parents had to go to work and there was no one who could take her. Her father **PROMISED** to take her that evening. So, Aabha spent the morning finishing her homework, slept in the afternoon, and then played. She waited eagerly for her father to come back.

Suddenly, the phone rang. It was her father and he told her that he would be late. Aabha was disappointed, but asked her father if she could go to the market without him. "Yes, but you must promise to be **careful**," said her father. Aabha promised, and set out.

Even though it was **RAINING**, the place was crowded. Aabha held her bag close to her and walked carefully through the **PUDDLES**. There were many stalls selling bedsheets, clothes, handicrafts, **jewellery** and more.

Aabha enjoyed walking through the narrow lanes and looking at all that was on sale. Her first stop was at the ice cream stall, where she treated herself to a large cone with five different **flavours!** She enjoyed her ice cream in the rain, and was looking around when she heard a loud voice.

"Personalised magic rings available here," yelled a shopkeeper with a big moustache and a large turban. "Come, get your **MAGIC** ring and see all your wishes come true!"

His words attracted Aabha. She walked closer. "Come and get your ring, little girl," he called out. "It's magic! Wear it and you will improve in studies, your enemies will become your friends, and all your problems will be solved!"

"I only want a ring that will help me get better **marks** 💯 in my exams," Aabha said, tempted.

"You've come to the right place," exclaimed the shopkeeper. "This is the best ring for you. Wear it, but remember, you need to recite your lessons three or four times a day, and this ring will guarantee **SUCCESS!** 👍 "

Aabha was convinced. She paid the man ₹20, took the ring, and went home. She wondered what she would tell her parents, but decided to keep quiet about it for now. She **slipped** the ring on her finger and began repeating all her lessons. She repeated them four times that day, and did the same for the next four days till her exams. She wrote her exams and waited impatiently for the results. When the report card came, Aabha had scored 90%. She was thrilled, and so were her parents.

"Ma, do you know why I did so well?" Aabha asked her mother that evening.

"I saw that you studied hard," replied her mother. "That would have got you good **marks!**"

"No, ma. It's because of this magic ring," said Aabha, showing her mother the ring.

"How does it work?" asked her mother, and Aabha explained what the shopkeeper told her.

"Hmmm…. So you wear the ring and repeat your **lessons** three or four times?" asked her mother.

"Yes," said Aabha, smiling at her report card.

"Aabha, it's not the ring. You memorised your lessons and your notes and made sure to repeat them. That's what helped you do well!" exclaimed her mother.

"You mean I spent more **time** studying because the shopkeeper told me that's what would make the ring work? So, it was my studying and not the ring?" asked Aabha.

Her mother nodded.

Aabha **grinned**, understanding what her mother was saying. Her hard work had paid off, and she didn't need magic rings to do well!

PUZZLE TIME

~~STRIKE OUT~~

Below are a few myths and truths, strike out the myths and circle the truths.

   a) Don't cut nails at night.

   b) Not chewing your food properly is unhealthy.

   c) You are lucky if you see a red car in the morning.

   d) A baby panda is smaller than a mouse at birth.

   e) If you call someone names, you become like them.

   f) Brushing your teeth twice daily is a healthy habit.

Answer on the last page

AVINASH CONQUERS HIS FEAR

By Navya Bhupathiraju

Avinash loved *singing* and practised daily with Mr Patel, his music teacher. However, he was scared of singing in front of anyone except Mr Patel and his mother. He was shy and never took part in any singing events.

His school was hosting its annual day. The organising committee thought it would be good to end the event with a **musical** performance. They told Mr Patel and asked him to begin auditions. The students were wildly excited about the audition, and jumped around waiting their turn. All except Avinash, who stood away from the crowd of children wanting to participate.

Mr Patel saw him and called him up. "Avinash, why aren't you joining the audition? You have a *beautiful* voice and will definitely be chosen!"

"Sorry, sir. My throat hurts," said Avinash weakly.

"Oh well, that's up to you. I think you'll do well," said Mr Patel.

Avinash admired Mr Patel and did not want to disappoint him.

"Sorry, sir. Will you put my name down for the audition, please?" he asked **NERVOUSLY.**

Mr Patel **smiled** and added his name to the list.

AVINASH'S EXCUSE TO ESCAPE

The audition began, and each student had to stand in front of the class and sing a part of a song. When it was Avinash's turn, he stood in front of the class nervously. He choked and could hardly **whisper** one line of a song. Luckily for him, the bell rang for lunch and Avinash ran back to his seat.

Before he could leave the class, Mr Patel asked him to stay back. "I'm sorry, sir. I simply could not sing," said Avinash sadly.

"Don't worry about it, Avinash. I understand that you get nervous in front of people but remember that you should not let fear ruin your **dreams** 的."

"But, sir, I am so scared to perform. I keep thinking 'What if I forget the words? What if no one likes the way I sing?'"

"I understand your **fear** but if you don't sing, you won't know. Once you sing, you will find the answers to your questions. I like the way you sing and I think you are one of the most **talented** students in this school," replied Mr Patel.

Avinash nodded, but he was still scared.

"How about I join you on **stage** on the annual day?" asked Mr Patel.

Avinash was relieved to hear that because now he wouldn't be performing alone. "That'll be **GREAT,** sir. When can we begin practising?"

"Tomorrow."

The two practised daily. Finally, on the day of the event, Avinash and Mr Patel came on stage and the audience cheered. Avinash was nervous. Mr Patel told him to only concentrate on the paper. Knowing that Mr Patel was by his side, Avinash and started singing alongwith Mr Patel.

As they started singing the second verse, Avinash got so immersed in the song with his eyes closed that he did not see Mr Patel leave the stage. He sang alone and completed the performance and when he opened his eyes he saw the audience standing and **CLAPPING**. Shocked, Avinash looked around him and saw Mr Patel standing with the audience, smiling at him.

Everyone cheered for Avinash, who was overwhelmed. He thanked everyone with a wide grin and understood why Mr Patel left the stage half way through. "Thank you, sir. Thank you for giving me the **courage**," he said fervently.

"This was you. The courage and talent were within you. They only had to be unleashed," replied Mr Patel. Avinash was no longer afraid to sing in front of everyone. He had **conquered** his fear.

WHERE iS BATASHA?

By Pankaj Roy

Potato was tired of **LOOKING** for Batasha, the sugar lump. "I don't understand this!" he exclaimed. "I simply cannot find Batasha. For the first time, I think I have to give up!" All the groceries in the kitchen were playing hide-and-seek, and Potato was the **seeker.**

"Ha ha ha. Ready to give up?" Potato heard the voice of Batasha, but could not find him anywhere.

Overhead, Lightbulb **grinned,** happy that Batasha was winning this game.

Why was Batasha teasing Potato? And why was Lightbulb happy about this? To answer that, let us go back a few weeks.

THiS iS HOW THE STORY BEGiNS

There was a **beautiful** guest house built atop a hill. In winters, it was full of families who came to ski and enjoy other winter sports, but in summer, it stood **empty.** The various items of food in the kitchen were bored and decided to play hide-and-seek. Batasha, Biscuit, Banana, Potato, and all the others on the grocery shelf found the game engrossing. But Batasha would always get caught first. Being white and round, he found it difficult to **hide**.

"...eight, nine, ten! Everyone hide because I'm coming!" shouted Banana, who was the seeker. He opened his eyes and **LOOKED** around the kitchen. There! There was a white blob behind the fridge. Banana sneaked up and peeped and sure enough, there was Batasha!

"Batasha, you're out! I see you behind the fridge," laughed Banana.

"Oh ho! Why am I always the first to be caught!" **EXCLAIMED** Batasha, coming out.

"Batasha will now **seek** and we will hide!" said Biscuit, laughing at Batasha's despair at being caught again.

"Batasha, you are really stupid," said proud Potato, who always made fun of Batasha. "Hide-and-seek is really not meant for such foolish people like you!" Potato never lost an **opportunity** to mock Batasha. This went on for some time.

One evening, Batasha was on his shelf, weeping softly. "What's the matter?" asked Water Glass.

WHEN BATASHA HIDES, NO ONE CAN FIND HIM

"The others make fun of me because I'm not able to hide well when we **play**," wept Batasha.

"Batasha, crying will not **solve** your problem. We need to use our brains. Let us think of how to solve this," said Glass. The two sat in silence for some time, thinking.

"I have an idea!" exclaimed Glass, and *whispered* his idea to Batasha.

"This is a brilliant plan!" exclaimed Batasha. "Your brain is excellent, Glass!"

The next day, when they began PLAYING, it was Potato's turn to be seeker. He shut his eyes and counted to ten. When he opened his eyes, he was sure he would find Batasha immediately. But there was no Batasha to be found! Potato searched high and low, but could not find Batasha. "Ready to give up?" came the mocking VOICE of Batasha. Potato was exhausted trying to find the lump of sugar. Finally, for the first time since they started playing hide-and-seek, Potato had to give up.

"Batasha, I give up," he said.

"Batasha, come on out! Potato has given up," shouted Biscuit, coming out from his hiding place behind some sacks.

"Where is he hiding?" WONDERED Banana.

"I'm hiding here in the glass in front of you," giggled Batasha. But still nobody could see him.

Finally, Glass explained. "You see, sugar dissolves in water. So, Batasha has dissolved himself in the water. That's why you can't see him."

Potato was STUNNED. He had been thoroughly defeated by science. Then Banana asked: "If you are dissolved, how are you going to come out, Batasha?"

Batasha and Glass laughed. "We have an answer to that," they said together. Glass then *walked* out into the sun and stood there for some time. The sun was hot and the water soon evaporated, leaving grains of sugar behind. Batasha put those grains together, and was soon his usual round, white self. Potato, Banana, and Biscuit were amazed. Only Lightbulb above was not **SURPRISED**. After all, he knew the whole story from the beginning!

93

🔍 Find Out

In which of these substances will sugar dissolve?

Answer on the last page

THE REAL VICTORY

By Poonam Mehta

Nicky the Rabbit loved **sports**. He was very fond of running and always stood first in races. In fact, he was called 'Junior Milkha Singh' in school. His parents were **PROUD** of his abilities and often spoke about him to friends and relatives.

This did not mean that Nicky neglected his lessons. He was a good student, and usually topped his class. Apart from this, he was very keen on extracurricular activities like dance and **drama**. As a result, Nicky was very popular in school and had a number of friends.

POPULAR NICKY GOT HIS COMPETITOR

One day, the teacher told them a new student was joining them. It was Raj the Rabbit, a good-looking but *shy* rabbit. It turned out that Raj was also very smart.

He always had a **SMILING** face, and was willing to help out at any time. Raj and Nicky shared so many interests, they soon became very good friends.

The Annual Sports Day was coming up, and the teacher allocated work to Raj and Nicky, who were among the most responsible in the class. Finally, the Sports Day arrived. There were many RACES and competitions including the relay race, short putt, lemon-and-spoon race, high jump, flat race, and tug-of-war.

WHO WILL WIN THE RACE?

The highlight was the **RUNNING** race, but this year, surprisingly, there were only a few participants. A number of students had fallen ill because of the changing weather. Nicky was surprised to see Raj step forward to take part in this race. After all, Raj had joined the school after the **SELECTION** rounds were over. But then he overheard a teacher say that if there had been even one less participant, they would have cancelled the race.

The participants took their places, and the **referee** shouted: "On your marks. Get set. Go!" As usual, Nicky took the lead. He noticed that Raj was able to keep up with him easily. The others had already fallen behind.

It looked like Raj was a good runner, and Nicky was afraid he would be beaten in this race. If Raj won, the entire school would **praise** him. Then what would happen to Nicky's popularity?

Nicky did not want that to happen and wanted to win at all costs. "Shall I blow **dust** in his eyes?" he thought, as he ran. "Or shall I slyly trip him so nobody will notice?"

But Nicky's conscience would not allow him to **WiN** in this manner. "I will simply do my best!" thought Nicky. "If Raj overtakes me, I just have to bear it!"

The two came to the final and most difficult stretch of the race. The race-track was uphill and **ROCKY** and Raj began to struggle. Nicky too found the race very tough, but he called up all his willpower and surged ahead. He could hear his friends screaming, "Buck up, Nicky!" These words of **encouragement** inspired him. Raj stumbled, but managed to keep up, and the two friends crossed the finish line together.

The entire school stood up to cheer for them. Nicky was **overwhelmed**, not because he won the race but because he had won over his wicked thoughts.

BECKY'S RIDDLING BIRTHDAY

By Swathi Suresh

Becky was seven years old. She lived with her mother, father, and older brother Tike in a **house**  on Park Street in Bengaluru. She went to Bridge's Higher Secondary School, which was close by, and went to school with her neighbour Pinky. Though Pinky was nine years old, the two were best friends.

It was Friday evening, and Becky and Pinky were **WALKING** home from school. Half way there, they met Tike. He was heading to the park to play with his friends. "Are you leaving me alone at home?" asked Becky.

"Oh, Pinky can stay with you! Can't you, Pinky?" he asked.

"Of course I will," said Pinky.

"Just make sure you stay **INDOORS** and shut the door behind you!" instructed Tike, and the two girls ran home happily. Once they reached, they made sure to shut the front door. As she was about to bolt it shut, Pinky exclaimed: "What's this?"

Becky turned around.

FIND WHAT IS HIDDEN IN THE RIDDLE

"Look! There's a note stuck to the door," said Pinky.

The two pulled down the sticky **NOTE.** Becky read it out loud:

"Hello there! Give me power and I can keep things cold and **FROZEN**.

Take it away from me and I can melt things easily.

Find me out and see what I have for you."

"Who put this riddle here?" Becky asked, **CONFUSED.**

"I don't know. But let's find out!" Pinky was excited.

"Alright. But what does this **RIDDLE** mean?" Becky asked.

"Think!" Pinky said. "What can keep things cold and melt it?"

Both of them stood there *thinking*☺. Then Becky shouted: "It's the fridge. A refrigerator keeps things cold when there's power and melts things when there's no power!"

The two ran to the **FRIDGE** and opened it. There was a big red box inside, tied with a beautiful white bow. "What's that?" Becky squeaked in excitement.

"Open it, open it," shouted Pinky, equally excited.

Becky pulled the bow open, and opened the box. Her mouth fell open when she saw the box was filled with **chocolates** of different shapes and colours. Becky's face flushed with

amazement and Pinky was too surprised to speak.

Then they found another note stuck to the **INSIDE** of the lid.

This time, Pinky pulled it out and read:

"I can show you anything you want.

Your favourite **cartoon** too.

Come to me and there is something for you!"

"The **TV**," Pinky answered instantly.

Both of them ran to the living room and there was a small rectangular package on top of the television. This too had a bow on it.

This box contained a small photo frame with a **lovely** photo of Becky and Pinky hugging each other.

"Is this your work? Are you giving me all these presents?" Becky asked Pinky.

"Oh no. When could I have done all this! After classes, I've been with you all the time," said Pinky.

"I **wonder** who could have done this," Becky said. "Look, there's another note behind the frame!"

This note said:

"You can see what I see,

If you find who I am,

Then, you have another **SURPRISE!**"

"What can this be?" wondered Becky.

Pinky and Becky both stood there thinking. Suddenly, Pinky exclaimed: "It's a mirror!"

The two ran to every **MIRROR** in the house but there was nothing anywhere. "Becky, is there a mirror in your parents' room?" asked Pinky.

Becky nodded, and the two ran there. Sure enough, there was a large parcel waiting for them. Pinky had to help Becky open the **box**, and there was a doll that Becky had wanted for months! Pinky pressed a red **button** on the doll's back, and it sang "Happy birthday".

"I had forgotten! It's my birthday tomorrow!" exclaimed Becky.

The two girls settled down to play with the doll. As they were playing, Becky noticed a tiny note tucked in the doll's shoe.

"If you feel sleepy, come to me.

I am soft and **fluffy**," she read.

"The bed!" Becky shouted in excitement.

They ran to Becky's room, and there on her bed was a huge **chocolate** cake, which had "Happy birthday, Becky!" written on it in pink icing.

"Time for the next riddle!" Pinky said.

"You think there's more?" Becky asked and Pinky **nodded**. She had spotted another note in the cake box. Pinky read it:

"If you **DROP** something,

What do you do to pick it up?"

Without thinking, both of them bent down to look under the **COT** at the same time. There it was—a blue package. Becky pulled it out and started removing the covers hastily. Inside was a pair of blue **shoes**. Becky had been asking her parents for these shoes for many months, and they had refused to buy them. And here they were—a **birthday** present!

"These are such pretty shoes!" said Pinky. She pulled out a note that was stuck inside the lid of the shoebox. It said, **"HAPPY BIRTHDAY, BECKY!"**

WHO IS AT THE DOOR TO WISH BECKY?

Just then, the doorbell rang and they went to open it. It was Becky's mother. They told her about all the **riddles** and showed her everything they found.

"Mother, do you know who did this? I first thought it was Pinky," said Becky.

Mother smiled and said, "The chocolates are from your brother, the photo is from Pinky's parents." Pinky looked **SURPRISED**. "The doll is from Grandfather, the cake from Grandmother and the shoes are from me and Father." She said, "Do you like your new shoes?"

"Mother, I **love** them!" Becky hugged and kissed her mother.

The next day, Becky had a birthday party with all her friends and family. But she told them all that the best **party** had been the day before, when she and Pinky had a riddling party!

PUZZLE TIME

RIDDLE ME OUT!

Becky received another gift from her parents. Read the clue below and help her guess what's inside the box.

Clue:

I am soft and cute,
I look handsome in a suit,
I can jump and run,
Together, we will have fun.

Answer on the last page

LET'S VISIT THE MOON

By Shams Al Farooqi

It was the last day of school. Sheela, the class teacher, was supposed to hand out the holiday homework. "Will the children play during the **holidays** or will they spend most of their time studying?" she thought to herself. Then she had an idea.

PLANNING FOR SUMMER HOLIDAYS

She looked up and asked the children: "What are you going to do in the holidays? How many of you know?" Most of the kids **raised** their hands. "That's good. So when you return to school after the holidays, I want all of you to write an essay about what you did and where you went."

"Yes, madam," said the **children** in unison.

"And remember, you will write the **essay** in Hindi!"

Again the children said: "Yes, madam." They couldn't say no, since Sheela was their Hindi teacher as well.

"So tell me, who is going where?" asked Sheela. A number of hands went up, but as she usually did, Sheela looked for the children who did not raise their hands. "Mukul," she called out to a boy in the last **row.** "What are your plans?"

"Mummy hasn't said anything yet," mumbled Mukul.

"Well, you tell her what you want to do, and if it is possible, I'm sure she will take you," she said *positively*.

"So, who will tell me where they want to go?" asked Sheela.

Sakshi jumped up before she was called and **anonced**: "I want to go to Mumbai."

"That's **NICE**," said Sheela. "What places are you going to visit in Mumbai? Do you know anything about Mumbai?"

"Yes, madam," replied Sakshi. "My uncle lives there. I want to see the **Arabian Sea**, Essel World, Film City, and the Taj Mahal."

A voice from the back of the class interrupted her saying, "The Taj Mahal isn't in Mumbai, you silly girl."

Sakshi immediately replied, "Yes, I know." She turned back and gave Harshith an **ANGRY** look.

"Who said 'silly girl'?" Sheela asked sternly.

Harshith stood up.

"Where are your manners? How can you talk to anyone so rudely?"

Harshith tried to defend himself. "But, teacher... the TAJ MAHAL is in Agra. I know it, as I have visited it."

IS THE TAJ MAHAL IN MUMBAI OR AGRA?

Sheela replied, "I know that as well. The Taj Mahal is also the name of a hotel in Mumbai. Sakshi must've heard of it. It is a famous hotel. Many people visit it."

"Yes, madam, you are right," replied Sakshi.

Actually, she was **confused** about the Taj Mahal in Mumbai and Agra. However, she automatically said yes to the teacher!

Sheela looked at another part of the class and asked, "Now who is going to tell me where they want to go? Avinash, why don't you tell me?"

Avinash stood up, but remained silent. Before she could question him, Bhaskar piped up. "Teacher, he wants to go to the moon. He just told me."

The whole class started **laughing**. Avinash kicked Bhaskar under the desk.

Sheela rapped on her desk to get the students to be silent.

LET'S PLAN A VACATION TO THE MOON!

"This is not a laughing matter. Why can't Avinash visit the moon? We should have strong ideas and wishes to fulfil them. You can definitely go and visit the moon, Avinash. Maybe not during this **vacation**, but you can definitely visit the moon some day."

Then Sheela decided to quiz Avinash. "Do you know how to travel to the moon?"

"Yes, madam," said Avinash eagerly. "We need to travel in a space 🪐 shuttle."

"Yes, you are right. But what is the Hindi word for that?" asked Sheela.

Avinash was silent, but Garvita **shouted** the answer. (She always shouted when she knew an answer. Nobody knew why.) "Antariksh Yaan."

Sheela looked encouragingly at Avinash. "I'm sure you knew that word."

Avinash nodded silently; he actually did not know the word, but did not want to disagree with his teacher!

"Do you know the name of the first man on the 🌑moon?" Sheela asked him.

Avinash stuttered. "Neil...no. Neela Haath Balwan!"

"What? Who is that?" demanded Sheela.

"Teacher, you asked for the Hindi word. I only know him as Neil Armstrong," said poor Avinash.

SING IN UNISON

Sheela didn't know whether to **LAUGH** or to cry! "No, Avinash, names remain the same in any language.

You should not translate names."

Avinash nodded, relieved.

"So why do you want to go to the moon, Avinash?" asked Sheela.

The reply was prompt: "To unfurl our country's **flag** ."

"To unfurl a flag?" Sheela wasn't expecting this answer. "You want to go to the moon just to unfurl a flag?"

"Yes, teacher," replied Avinash. "Whenever we see a picture of the moon in our textbooks, every PICTURE shows the American flag on it. I will go to the moon, add the Indian flag and come back."

Sheela looked thoughtfully at Avinash. This was true patriotism, she thought. In fact, it INSPIRED her to ask the class: "Shall we sing Vande Mataram? Do you all know the words?"

The students all rose to their feet and began **Singing** with her: "Sujalam Sufalam Malayaja Sheetalam Shasyashyamalan Mataram... Vande Mataram!"

3-D FILM

By Vivek Chakravarty

Kapil the Mouse was in a very good mood. He was going to watch a movie.

He cycled to the theatre and walked in cheerfully. "One ticket for a balcony seat please," he asked the mouse selling tickets. The ticket seller handed him a ticket and a pair of **glasses** 👓 .

"I don't need glasses!" exclaimed Kapil, but there was a long queue for tickets and the mouse at the counter had no time to answer.

KAPIL'S FIRST 3D FILM

Kapil was puzzled, and as he walked into the hall, he asked the ticket checker: "What am I supposed to do with these strange glasses?"

"Sir, you need to wear them while watching the **movie** 🎥," said the ticket checker.

"I can see very well!" EXCLAIMED Kapil. "I don't need glasses."

"Oh, sir, these are special 3-D glasses. Do wear them when the movie starts," was the advice he got.

Kapil was not at all sure about this, but decided to follow the ticket checker's suggestion and put on the glasses when the movie began.

"Wow! I feel like I'm a part of what's going on!" thought Kapil, enjoying the movie where mice were Chasing a villain cat through the city. Suddenly, the cat jumped towards Kapil. "Help! A cat! Run for your lives! Cat in the hall!" screamed Kapil, trying to scramble out of his seat. The other mice too PANICKED when they heard this. They all ran helter-skelter, trying to run away from the cat.

The movie was stopped and the security guards rushed in. "Where is this cat? Who saw it?" they demanded.

THE CAT IS ON SCREEN

"It was a large grey cat with a red tie," squeaked Kapil. "It JUMPED straight at me!"

"He thought the movie cat was real!" exclaimed Amar the Mouse, who had also come to watch the film. All the mice began **LAUGHING**.

"No, it was a real cat!" insisted Kapil. "A movie cat could not have jumped straight at me!"

"That's the beauty of a 3-D movie," explained Amar. "It is made so that you **feel** as if you are in the scene or as if the characters are around you."

"How is this possible?" asked a confused Kapil.

"Is this the first 3-D movie you've seen?" asked Chatur the Mouse, who worked in the **theatre.**

"Yes," admitted Kapil.

"That's why he thought the cat was real!" exclaimed a mouse sitting in the back row. "We all felt like that the first time we saw a 3-D movie."

"But how do they make the **characters** jump out of the screen?" asked Kapil.

Chatur tried to explain. "In a regular movie, you only see things in two dimensions, that is, width and height. In a 3-D movie, they add a third dimension, which is **depth**. So things seem real and as if they are coming at us," he said.

"So do they **shoot** the movies differently?"

"The cameras used are different," said Chatur. "To make a 3-D film, two cameras are joined in such a manner that the distance between their **lenses** is the same as that between our eyes. But that alone isn't enough. Once the film is made, you need special projection hardware to see it properly. That's why you are given these special glasses."

"Oh, now I understand why I was given these glasses!" exclaimed Kapil. "I tried explaining to everyone that my **⊚sight⊚** was fine!" All the mice laughed at this.

"If you had seen a 3-D movie some years before, you would have been given glasses with one red lens and one blue or green lens," said Chatur, grinning.

"Why? That sounds like part of a clown's costume!" exclaimed Kapil.

"You see, the different coloured lenses would trick the brain. Each eye sees a different coloured image which combine in the brain. If you watch a 3-D movie without these glasses, the IMAGES will be very blurry," explained Chatur.

"But these glasses are not red and blue," pointed out Kapil.

"Yes. Technology has advanced and we now use what are called polarised lenses. These lenses filter horizontal and vertical light waves to make you see depth in the images. The images you see with these glasses are much crisper and clearer than with the coloured glasses," said Chatur.

Kapil was FASCINATED. "I think I need to do a lot more research on 3-D movies," he said. "But for now, let's start the movie again and see if that cat is caught!"

Everyone laughed, and settled down to watch the lifelike movie.

PUZZLE TIME

DO IT YOURSELF

Follow the instructions below and make your own 3-D glasses.

You need: old transparent glasses, red and blue permanent markers

Step 1: Colour the right eye area with the blue marker.

Step 2: Colour the left eye area with the red marker.

YOUR SNAZZY 3-D GLASSES ARE READY!

TOOTHLESS WANTS TO BE PERFECT

By Vidya JS

Toothless the Shark was posing in front of a shiny shell. He looked at his reflection and sighed. "I wish I was perfect," he said sadly. The fish on the MOVIE 🎬 posters he loved were colourful and bright, especially the orange clownfish.

"I wish I was orange like the clownfish," he said to his mum one day.

"Orange? My goodness, whoever heard of an orange shark," she laughed. "But why orange in particular?"

PERFECTION IS ALL TOOTHLESS NEEDS

"I want to be perfect," said Toothless.

"Orange is not our COLOUR, dear. You will just look ill. Sharks are grey. And you are a dashing grey," she said.

Toothless thought that movie stars had to look **PERFECT**. He had been reading a lot of articles and realised that fish were made to look very different from real life with the aid of technology. Maybe the clownfish was not so **handsome**, or so orange, after all.

"So how does one become perfect, if not by copying movie stars?" he wondered **ALOUD** to Finfin, his little sister. Finfin did not have the answer, so she asked a question: "But why do you want to be perfect?"

"Because being perfect is the perfect thing to be," he replied.

He decided to ask his cousin, Hammerhead the Shark. "Hammy, I want to be perfect."

Hammy **thought** for a moment and said with authority: "Let's go and see Dr Crab. He has all the answers. He has just written a book, 'How to be happy, not crabby'. It's a No. 1 bestseller."

"Really? I do hope he knows how to make a shark perfect."

Dr Crab was a busy crustacean. But Hammy got an appointment.

On the given day, Toothless was very nervous. He thought about his **big** teeth and grey body and wondered if he ever would be perfect. He mustered up his courage and swam to Dr Crab's cave. He spotted a tiny crab resting on a rock. He seemed to be sleeping.

"Hello, I'm Toothless."

No answer.

"Ahem… If you please, Dr Crab, I would like to be perfect."

Silence.

"Hello?" asked Toothless after a long time.

"Come back tomorrow," yelled Dr Crab.

Toothless shook at the loud voice and **swam** away. He came back the next day.

"Ah, I wanted to check if you are serious. Only serious people can be perfect. Now listen carefully. You have three tasks to complete," said Dr Crab, when he saw Toothless again.

"The first task—wear **seaweed** on your head for a whole day."

"But…"

"No buts… Just do as I say, if you wish to be perfect," said Dr Crab.

Toothless found some seaweed and placed it on his head. Everyone **laughed**. But Toothless kept it on.

The next day when he went back, Dr Crab said, "Collect a thousand shells."

Toothless searched **HIGH** and low for shells. He was exhausted. But he did it. He

took the pile in his enormous mouth and placed it near Dr Crab's **cave.**

"Hmm… I will have my assistants count it. Does it have any conch shells in it? They are my favourite."

There was not one word of appreciation from Dr Crab and Toothless was a little disappointed. But he was quiet.

"Next, say bye to all your silly imperfect friends. Perfect **CREATURES** should only be with other perfect creatures like me."

"But you live alone," blurted out Toothless. He couldn't live without his silly friends and family.

"Everyone can't be perfect? It does get lonely at the top… err… bottom of the ocean sometimes. But hey, I'm perfect."

Toothless nodded. He was beginning to think being perfect was not such a perfect idea after all.

"Okay, I will give up my friends," he said.

"Here you go then. Here is your certificate," Dr Crab *welcomed* him to the perfect club.

"Toothless has passed the three levels. He is now perfect in every way" – it read.

Toothless took his certificate and went **HOME** 🏠. He did feel perfect now that he had the certificate, but did not feel happy.

"Why are you sad?" asked Finfin.

"I'm not sad. I'm perfect. Can't you see the difference?" he snapped.

His little sister did not like her brother so quiet and boring. She wanted the one who always cracked jokes, worried that his teeth were too big, and helped others in times of need. She missed all the times they played together. But Toothless said that because he was perfect now, he could not behave in a silly manner.

SILLY TOOTHLESS LOSES HIS FRIENDS

His friends also got tired of asking him to come out and PLAY. "What's the point of being perfect, if you can't do anything?" asked Hammy, shaking his fins.

Finally, Toothless had enough. He went back to Dr Crab one day and met him.

"Well, how is it going, CHAMP?" Dr Crab asked.

"I think being perfect is boring."

"You are a lovely young shark. Look at all the things you did. You swam with seaweed on your head for a whole day. And though people laughed, you did not care what they thought."

"You collected a thousand shells. By doing this task without complaining, you showed that you had focus and perseverance."

Toothless beamed.

"And thirdly, without your friends and family to be silly with, you saw that life isn't worth that much. Why try to be perfect? Just be yourself," said Dr Crab, with a **twinkle** in his eyes.

Toothless swam home merrily. He made faces at everyone he met. Cracked jokes with the jellyfish; hung out with Hammy; played **GAMES** with Finfin; and helped the baby turtles reach home after school.

"I am perfectly happy being Toothless," he declared. His sister clapped her hands in delight.

"We **LOVE** you just the way you are," said everybody.

Dr Crab was a very clever crab after all.

WAY TOO SWEET

By S. Varalakshmi

Rishi the Bear was sitting alone, looking sad.

"Why the **long** face, Rishi?" asked Kittu the Wolf.

"I'm on a diet," said Rishi dully.

"Why?" asked Kittu.

"My mother wants me to take part in a running race in two months. I have to lose weight to *RUN* fast, so I'm only allowed to eat berries and no honey. How can a bear live without honey? I wish I could eat just one jar a day and not any more," said Rishi sadly.

"A jar a day? That is way too much!" **EXCLAIMED** Kittu.

"Will you please go to Deedee the Deer's shop and buy me a jar of honey?" pleaded Rishi.

"Why can't you go?" asked Kittu.

"Ma has warned Deedee not to sell me **HONEY.**"

Kittu laughed, and Rishi scowled at him.

Kittu apologised and then said, "Maybe you should find a job to keep your mind **distracted**."

"I don't think that will help. When I worked as a baker's assistant, I put on a lot of **weight**. And I don't know anything else except baking," said Rishi.

"I will give you a job," said a voice.

SURPRISED, Rishi and Kittu turned around and saw Furu the Fox walking towards them.

"Were you eavesdropping all this time?" asked Kittu, suspiciously.

"I am too cool to do something like that. But I can't help it if you were a bit **loud**," retorted Furu.

"Could you tell me more about the job?" asked Rishi, brushing aside Kittu's question.

"I am looking for a cook and will pay ₹3,500 a month. Are you interested?" asked Furu.

"Yes! I will begin tomorrow," said an **overjoyed** Rishi.

"Are you sure, Rishi? You could look for a job elsewhere…" said Kittu, who didn't trust Furu at all.

FOR RiSHi, COOKiNG iS FUN

Rishi reassured Kittu and the next day, arrived at Furu's house

in the morning.

Furu greeted him and took him to the kitchen. He opened the cabinets and showed Rishi where the spices, **SUGAR**, honey, and flour were kept.

"You will find all the ingredients that you need here. If not, do ask me," said Furu.

Rishi just stared at the **JARS** of honey with his mouth open.

"Now, let's see how you stick to your diet, you big ball of fur," thought Furu. His aim was to make Rishi break his diet and then make fun of him when he could not run in the race.

"What shall I make?" asked Rishi, staring at the honey.

"Hmmm…. I think I'll have a honey lemon tea with honey butter croissants for breakfast," said Furu with an evil grin. "Can you make those?"

Rishi nodded and started work. Furu went to watch **television**, but his mind was not on the programme. He had deliberately asked for food that had honey, and was sure Rishi would give in to temptation and eat the honey.

Meanwhile, Rishi had put on his apron and chef's hat and had started cooking. The **scent** of honey was tempting, but he had promised his mother he would not eat honey, so he gritted his teeth and did not even taste a drop. Furu couldn't contain himself and **sneaked** up to the kitchen door to see what was happening. He saw Rishi squeezing lemons for the tea, and from the oven came the most **delicious** scent of croissants baking. Furu's tummy growled in hunger as he inhaled the delicious aroma. The sly fox hid near the kitchen for a long time, but Rishi concentrated on cooking and didn't eat any honey.

Disappointed and **HUNGRY**, Furu sneaked back to the living room.

Rishi soon set things on the trolley and served Furu.

"Please try these and let me know if you want me to change anything," said Rishi.

Furu **sipped** the tea and then had a bite of the croissant and quickly cleaned the plate.

"I have never tasted anything so delicious," he said, licking his lips. "For lunch, I would like you to make naan and honey chilli potatoes, and for **dessert** ☺, I want honey ice cream. Could you also bake a honey cake and honey biscuits with some more honey lemon tea?" asked Furu, not giving up on his plan to tempt Rishi.

Rishi **nodded** and went back to the kitchen.

After such a heavy breakfast, Furu felt drowsy and fell asleep on the couch.

At 1 p.m., Rishi woke him up.

"I have cooked everything that you asked for. I have prepared **dinner** too. I will leave for the day and come tomorrow," said Rishi and left.

Furu uncovered the lids and looked at the most **exotic** dishes he had seen. His mouth was watering and he wondered where Rishi had learned to cook so well.

Even though he wasn't hungry after eating a heavy breakfast, the food in front of him was so tempting, he simply had to eat! He decided he would have a single helping of each dish, but ended up eating everything.

Never had he eaten so much! Clutching his overstuffed **belly,** he lay down on the couch and went back to sleep.

This became his routine for the next few weeks. Soon, Furu had put on a lot of weight, but he couldn't stop eating what Rishi cooked. He kept ordering more and more dishes with honey, thinking that Rishi would be tempted, but Rishi stuck to his promise of not eating **honey.**

ALWAYS HAVE FUN, BUT WiTH CARE

One day, Furu saw himself in the mirror and was shocked.

"When did I put on so much weight?"

Just then Rishi entered with honey bread, looking slim and fit. "Here is the honey bread that you asked for. Hope you like it. This **time**, I added extra honey. Also, all 20 jars of honey are empty. Shall I go and buy more?" he asked.

Furu was shocked. That was his annual store of honey. He had managed to eat it all in a few weeks! Thinking of that, he picked up a piece of bread and **popped** it into his mouth. As he was chewing, he fainted.

Rishi rushed Furu to the doctor immediately. After examining him, the doctor said Furu's blood sugar levels were very high.

Hearing this, Furu had to hold himself from fainting again. He realised that his evil thoughts of making Rishi fat had backfired. Not only had Rishi kept his **PROMISE** to his mother, he had become fit by doing hard work in the kitchen.

Furu realised Rishi would easily win the *race*. He decided to stop tormenting people for no reason. Furu then told Rishi he would no longer require a cook. "From today, it's my turn to go on a diet!" he announced sadly.